BEWARE!

ALSO BY R.L. STINE

BEWARE!

R.L. STINE

PICKS HIS FAVORITE SCARY STORIES

Avon Books

An Imprint of HarperCollins*Publishers*

PARACHUTE

Beware!
Copyright © 2002 by Parachute Publishing, L.L.C.
Book design by Archie Ferguson
Library of Congress Cataloging-in-Publication Data
Beware!: R.L. Stine picks his favorite scary stories / by R.L. Stine.
p. cm.
A Parachute Press book.
Summary: A selection of unsettling stories by such authors as Ray Bradbury,
William Sleator, Leon Garfield, Roald Dahl, Gahan Wilson, and Mr. Stine himself.
ISBN 0-06-623842-0 — ISBN 0-06-623843-9 (lib. bdg.)
ISBN 0-06-055547-5 (pbk.)
1. Horror tales, American. 2. Horror tales, English. 3. Children's stories,
American. 4. Children's stories, English. [1. Horror stories. 2. Short stories.] I. Stine, R.L.
PZ5.B43428 2002   2002018938
[Fic]—dc21   CIP
                                                                                              AC
First Avon edition, 2004
AVON TRADEMARK REG. U.S. PAT. OFF. AND IN OTHER COUNTRIES,
MARCA REGISTRADA, HECHO EN U.S.A.
❖
Visit us on the World Wide Web!
www.harperchildrens.com

FOR RAY BRADBURY AND JACK DAVIS

With grateful thanks for all the pleasure your
work has given me and for the honor of
including some of it in this book.

CONTENTS

BEWARE!

THE BLACK FERRIS

by Ray Bradbury

ILLUSTRATED BY JOHN JUDE PALENCAR

When I was nine or ten years old, I discovered the stories of Ray Bradbury, and they changed my life. The stories were so scary, so funny, so surprising—and so beautifully written—I couldn't read enough of them. Ray Bradbury turned me into a reader.

To this day, I always tell people that the creepiest book I ever read was Bradbury's book about an evil carnival, *Something Wicked This Way Comes*. Imagine my surprise when I found this short story, "The Black Ferris." Bradbury liked it so much, he later expanded it into the novel. But as you will see, the story is a chilling ride on its own. . . .

THE
BLACK FERRIS

by Ray Bradbury

The carnival had come to town like an October wind, like a dark bat flying over the cold lake, bones rattling in the night, mourning, sighing, whispering up the tents in the dark rain. It stayed on for a month by the gray, restless lake of October, in the black weather and increasing storms and leaden skies.

During the third week, at twilight on a Thursday, the two small boys walked along the lakeshore in the cold wind.

"Aw, I don't believe you," said Peter.

"Come on, and I'll show you," said Hank.

They left wads of spit behind them all along the moist brown sand of the crashing shore. They ran to the lonely carnival grounds. It had been raining. The carnival lay by the sounding lake with nobody buying tickets from the flaky black booths, nobody hoping to get the salted hams from the whining roulette wheels, and none of the thin-fat freaks on the big platforms. The midway was silent, all the gray tents hissing on the wind like gigantic prehistoric wings. At eight o'clock perhaps, ghastly lights would flash on, voices would shout, music would go out over the lake. Now there was only a blind hunchback sitting on a black booth, feeling of the cracked china cup from which he was drinking some perfumed brew.

"There," said Hank, pointing.

The black Ferris wheel rose like an immense light-bulbed constellation against the cloudy sky, silent.

"I still don't believe what you said about it," said Peter.

"You wait, I saw it happen. I don't know how, but it did. You know how carnivals are; all funny. Okay; this one's even *funnier*."

Peter let himself be led to the high green hiding place of a tree.

Suddenly, Hank stiffened. "*Hist!* There's Mr. Cooger, the carnival man, now!" Hidden, they watched.

Mr. Cooger, a man of some thirty-five years, dressed in sharp bright clothes, a lapel carnation, hair greased with oil, drifted under the tree, a brown derby hat on his head. He had arrived in town three weeks before, shaking his brown derby hat at people on the street from inside his shiny red Ford, tooting the horn.

Now Mr. Cooger nodded at the little blind hunchback, spoke a word. The hunchback blindly, fumbling, locked Mr. Cooger into a black seat and sent him whirling up into the ominous twilight sky. Machinery hummed.

"See!" whispered Hank. "The Ferris wheel's going the wrong way. Backward instead of forward!"

"So what?" said Peter.

"Watch!"

The black Ferris wheel whirled twenty-five times around. Then the blind hunchback put out his pale hands and halted the machinery. The Ferris wheel stopped, gently swaying, at a certain black seat.

A ten-year-old boy stepped out. He walked off across the whispering carnival ground, in the shadows.

Peter almost fell from his limb. He searched the Ferris wheel with his eyes. "Where's Mr. Cooger?"

Hank poked him. "You wouldn't believe! Now *see*!"

"Where's Mr. Cooger at!"

"Come on, quick, run!" Hank dropped and was sprinting before he hit the ground.

Under giant chestnut trees, next to the ravine, the lights were burning in Mrs. Foley's white mansion. Piano music tinkled. Within the warm windows people moved. Outside, it began to rain, despondently, irrevocably, forever and ever.

"I'm *so* wet," grieved Peter, crouching in the bushes. "Like someone squirted me with a hose. How much longer do we wait?"

"Ssh!" said Hank, cloaked in wet mystery.

They had followed the little boy from the Ferris wheel up

through town, down dark streets to Mrs. Foley's ravine house. Now, inside the warm dining room of the house, the strange little boy sat at dinner, forking and spooning rich lamb chops and mashed potatoes.

"I know his name," whispered Hank quickly. "My mom told me about him the other day. She said, 'Hank, you hear about the li'l orphan boy moved in Mrs. Foley's? Well, his name is Joseph Pikes and he just came to Mrs. Foley's one day about two weeks ago and said how he was an orphan run away and could he have something to eat, and him and Mrs. Foley been getting on like hot apple pie ever since.' That's what my mom said," finished Hank, peering through the steamy Foley window. Water dripped from his nose. He held on to Peter, who was twitching with cold. "Pete, I didn't like his looks from the first, I didn't. He looked—mean."

"I'm scared," said Peter, frankly wailing. "I'm cold and hungry and I don't know what this's all about."

"Gosh, you're dumb!" Hank shook his head, eyes shut in disgust. "Don't you see, three weeks ago the carnival came. And about the same time this little ole orphan shows up at Mrs. Foley's. And Mrs. Foley's son died a long time ago one night one winter, and she's never been the same, so here's this little ole orphan boy who butters her all around."

"Oh," said Peter, shaking.

"Come on," said Hank. They marched to the front door and banged the lion knocker.

After a while the door opened and Mrs. Foley looked out.

"You're all wet, come in," she said. "My land." She herded them into the hall. "What do you want?" she said, bending over them, a tall lady with lace on her full bosom and a pale thin face with white hair over it. "You're Henry Walterson, aren't you?"

Hank nodded, glancing fearfully at the dining room, where the strange little boy looked up from his eating. "Can we see you alone, ma'am?" And when the old lady looked palely surprised, Hank crept over and shut the hall door and whispered at her. "We got to warn you about something, it's about that boy come to live with you, that orphan?"

The hall grew suddenly cold. Mrs. Foley drew herself high and stiff. "Well?"

"He's from the carnival, and he ain't a boy, he's a man, and he's planning on living here with you until he finds where your money is and then run off with it some night, and people will look for him but because they'll be looking for a little ten-year-old boy, they won't recognize him when he walks by a thirty-five-year-old man named Mr. Cooger!" cried Hank.

"What *are* you talking about?" declared Mrs. Foley.

"The carnival and the Ferris wheel and this strange man, Mr. Cooger, the Ferris wheel going backward and making him younger, I don't know how, and him coming here as a boy, and you can't trust him, because when he has your money he'll get on the Ferris wheel and it'll go *forward*, and he'll be thirty-five years old again, and the boy'll be gone forever!"

"Good night, Henry Walterson, don't *ever* come back!" shouted Mrs. Foley.

The door slammed. Peter and Hank found themselves in the rain once more. It soaked into and into them, cold and complete.

"Smart guy," snorted Peter. "Now you fixed it. Suppose he heard us, suppose he comes and *kills* us in our beds tonight, to shut us all up for keeps!"

"He wouldn't do that," said Hank.

"Wouldn't he?" Peter seized Hank's arm. "Look."

In the big bay window of the dining room now, the mesh curtain pulled aside. Standing there in the pink light, his hand made into a menacing fist, was the little orphan boy. His face was horrible to see, the teeth bared, the eyes hateful, the lips mouthing out terrible words. That was all. The orphan boy was there only a second, then gone. The curtain fell into place. The rain poured down upon the house. Hank and Peter walked slowly home in the storm.

During supper, Father looked at Hank and said, "If you don't catch pneumonia, I'll be surprised. Soaked, you were, by God! What's this about the carnival?"

Hank fussed at his mashed potatoes, occasionally looking at the rattling windows. "You know Mr. Cooger, the carnival man, Dad?"

"The one with the pink carnation in his lapel?" asked Father.

"Yes!" Hank sat up. "You've seen him around?"

"He stays down the street at Mrs. O'Leary's boardinghouse, got a room in the back. Why?"

"Nothing," said Hank, his face glowing.

After supper, Hank put through a call to Peter on the phone. At the other end of the line, Peter sounded miserable with coughing.

"Listen, Pete!" said Hank. "I see it all now. When that li'l ole orphan boy, Joseph Pikes, gets Mrs. Foley's money, he's got a good plan."

"What?"

"He'll stick around town as the carnival man, living in a room at Mrs. O'Leary's. That way nobody'll get suspicious of him. Everybody'll be looking for that nasty little boy and he'll be gone. And he'll be walking around all disguised as the carnival man. That way, nobody'll suspect the carnival at all. It would look funny if the carnival suddenly pulled up stakes."

"Oh," said Peter, sniffling.

"So we got to act fast," said Hank.

"Nobody'll believe us. I tried to tell my folks but they said hogwash!" moaned Peter.

"We got to act tonight, anyway. Because why? Because he's gonna try to kill us! We're the only ones that know and if we tell the police to keep an eye on him, he's the one who stole Mrs.

BEWARE!

Foley's money in cahoots with the orphan boy, he won't live peaceful. I bet he just tries something tonight. So, I tell you, meet me at Mrs. Foley's in half an hour."

"Aw," said Peter.

"You wanna die?"

"No." Thoughtfully.

"Well, then. Meet me there and I bet we see that orphan boy sneaking out with the money, tonight, and running back down to the carnival grounds with it, when Mrs. Foley's asleep. I'll see you there. So long, Pete!"

"Young man," said Father, standing behind him as he hung up the phone. "You're not going anywhere. You're going straight up to bed. Here." He marched Hank upstairs. "Now hand me out everything you got on." Hank undressed. "There're no other clothes in your room, are there?" asked Father.

"No, sir, they're all in the hall closet," said Hank disconsolately.

"Good," said Dad, and shut and locked the door.

Hank stood there, naked. "Holy cow," he said.

"Go to bed," said Father.

Peter arrived at Mrs. Foley's house at about nine-thirty, sneezing, lost in a vast raincoat and mariner's cap. He stood like a small water hydrant on the street, mourning softly over his fate. The lights in the Foley house were warmly on upstairs.

Peter waited for a half an hour, looking at the rain-drenched slick streets of night.

Finally, there was a darting paleness, a rustle in wet bushes.

"Hank?" Peter questioned the bushes.

"Yeah." Hank stepped out.

"Gosh," said Peter, staring. "You're—you're *naked*!"

"I ran all the way," said Hank. "Dad wouldn't let me out."

"You'll get pneumonia," said Peter.

The lights in the house went out.

"Duck," cried Hank, bounding behind some bushes. They waited. "Pete," said Hank. "You're wearing pants, aren't you?"

"Sure," said Pete.

"Well, you're wearing a raincoat, and nobody'll know, so lend me your pants," said Hank.

A reluctant transaction was made. Hank pulled the pants on.

The rain let up. The clouds began to break apart.

In about ten minutes, a small figure emerged from the house, bearing a large paper sack filled with some enormous loot or other.

"There he is," whispered Hank.

"There he goes!" cried Peter.

The orphan boy ran swiftly.

"Get after him!" cried Hank.

They gave chase through the chestnut trees, but the orphan boy was swift, up the hill, through the night streets of town, down past the rail yards, past the factories, to the midway of the deserted carnival. Hank and Peter were poor seconds, Peter weighted as he was with the heavy raincoat and Hank frozen with cold. The thumping of Hank's bare feet sounded through the town.

"Hurry, Pete! We can't let him get to that Ferris wheel before we do. If he changes back into a man, we'll never prove anything!"

"I'm hurrying!" But Pete was left behind as Hank thudded on alone in the clearing weather.

"Yah!" mocked the orphan boy, darting away, no more than a shadow ahead, now. Now vanishing into the carnival yard.

Hank stopped at the edge of the carnival lot. The Ferris wheel was going up and up into the sky, a big nebula of stars caught on the dark earth and turning forward and forward, instead of backward, and there sat Joseph Pikes in a black-painted bucket seat, laughing up and around and down and up and around and down at little old Hank standing there, and the little blind hunchback had his hand on the roaring, oily black machine that made the Ferris wheel go ahead and ahead. The midway was deserted because of the rain. The merry-go-round was still, but its music played and crashed in the open spaces. And Joseph Pikes rode up into the cloudy sky and came down, and each time he went around he was a year older, his laughing changed, grew deep, his face changed, the bones of it, the mean eyes of it, the wild hair of it, sitting there in the black bucket seat whirling, whirling swiftly, laughing into the bleak heavens where now and again a last split of lightning showed itself.

Hank ran forward at the hunchback by the machine. On the way he picked up a tent spike. "Here now!" yelled the hunchback. The black Ferris wheel whirled around. "You!" stormed the hunchback, fumbling out. Hank hit him in the kneecap and danced away. "Ouch!" screamed the man, falling forward. He tried to reach the machine brake to stop the Ferris wheel. When he put his hand on the brake, Hank ran in and slammed the tent spike against his fingers, mashing them. He hit them twice. The man held his hand in his other hand, howling. He kicked at Hank. Hank grabbed the foot, pulled, the man slipped in the mud and fell. Hank hit him on the head, shouting.

The Ferris wheel went around and around and around.

"Stop, stop the wheel!" cried Joseph Pikes-Mr. Cooger, flung up in a stormy cold sky in the bubbled constellation of whirl and rush and wind.

"I can't move," groaned the hunchback. Hank jumped on his chest and they thrashed, biting, kicking.

"Stop, stop the wheel!" cried Mr. Cooger, a man, a different man and voice this time, coming around in panic, going up into the roaring hissing sky of the Ferris wheel. The wind blew through the high dark wheel spokes. "Stop, stop, oh, please stop the wheel!"

BEWARE!

Hank leaped up from the sprawled hunchback. He started in on the brake mechanism, hitting it, jamming it, putting chunks of metal in it, tying it with rope, now and again hitting at the crawling weeping dwarf.

"Stop, stop, stop the wheel!" wailed a voice high in the night, where the windy moon was coming out of the vaporous white clouds now. "Stop . . ." The voice faded.

Now the carnival was ablaze with sudden light. Men sprang out of tents, came running. Hank felt himself jerked into the air with oaths and beatings rained on him. From a distance there was a sound of Peter's voice and behind Peter, at full tilt, a police officer with pistol drawn.

"Stop, stop the wheel!" In the wind the voice sighed away.

The voice repeated and repeated.

The dark carnival men tried to apply the brake. Nothing happened. The machine hummed and turned the wheel around and around. The mechanism was jammed.

"Stop!" cried the voice one last time.

Silence.

Without a word the Ferris wheel flew in a circle, a high system of electric stars and metal and seats. There was no sound now but the sound of the motor, which died and stopped. The Ferris wheel coasted for a minute, all the carnival people looking up at it, the policeman looking up at it, Hank and Peter looking up at it.

16

The Ferris wheel stopped. A crowd had gathered at the noise. A few fishermen from the wharf house, a few switchmen from the rail yards. The Ferris wheel stood whining and stretching in the wind.

"Look," everybody said.

The policeman turned and the carnival people turned and the fishermen turned and they all looked at the occupant in the black-painted seat at the bottom of the ride. The wind touched and moved the black wooden seat in a gentle rocking rhythm, crooning over the occupant in the dim carnival light.

A skeleton sat there, a paper bag of money in its hands, a brown derby hat on its head.

THE CONJURE BROTHER

by Patricia McKissack

ILLUSTRATED BY BRIAN PINKNEY

Ever wish you could have a new brother or sister? In this story, Josie is so desperate for a brother, she goes to see a conjure woman.

Not long ago, just about every small Southern farm town had a conjure woman. A woman who helped people by making strange potions and casting spells.

A lot of people didn't believe in the conjure woman's powers. But when Josie's new brother suddenly appears, Josie believes—she *really* believes!

Patricia McKissack writes beautifully about kids living in the rural South. I like this story because it changes directions several times. You think it's about one thing—but it surprises you by being about something else.

Patricia McKissack has written many prize-winning books and stories, and this is one of my creepy favorites.

THE
CONJURE BROTHER

by Patricia McKissack

Until recently, most rural Southern towns had a resident conjure woman who sold her knowledge of the powers of roots and herbs for donations of food or clothing. Though some people laughed at the conjure woman's spells and potions, others swore by her ability to change luck or cure an ailment. Every now and then a conjure woman came along whose powers transcended those of the ordinary "root doctors." There was no limit to what she could do.

Josie was tired of being the only child in the Hudson family. Her friends JoBeth and Arthur Lee had lots of brothers and sisters between them. Josie wanted a brother.

"I'm the girl in the family," she reasoned. "Wouldn't it be nice to have a boy? Then I could be the sister and he could be the brother. What do you think?" Josie asked her mother.

Mama always had a ready answer. "I forgot to let the stork know we moved from Kennerly Street to Harrison Avenue last year," she said, taking plates down from the cabinet. Josie set the

21

table. Mama smiled, then winked playfully. "So you see, he doesn't know where to bring a baby."

Josie knew better. Arthur Lee had told her and JoBeth how babies came into the world. "When your mother and father want a new baby, first your mama has to get fat," he'd said confidently. "She eats and eats until it looks like she's going to pop. But she doesn't. She goes to the hospital to lose the weight. Then they get to choose a baby. That's how it works."

Weeks passed and Mama stayed skinny. "She chews on celery," Josie told Arthur Lee and JoBeth at the sandbox. "I'll never get a brother."

"Well, my mama is big as a refrigerator," said Arthur Lee. "They say she'll be going to the hospital soon. If she brings home another baby boy, you can have him. I got four brothers, and that's enough!"

JoBeth added, "I saw in a magazine that you can adopt a baby from a faraway country for pennies a day."

No, Josie decided. "I want a brother that's the same as me."

"You don't always get what you want," Arthur Lee said. "Look at me."

"When my mother goes to the hospital, I'm going along to make sure they choose a brother."

Summer was passing quickly, and Mama was as thin as ever, snacking on carrot sticks. How could she get fat that way? Just when Josie was about to give up hope, she overheard Miz Annie and Miz Charlene talking about a conjure woman who had just moved to town.

"Reckon she could do something to change this streak of bad luck I been having?" Miz Annie asked.

Miz Charlene answered, "Yes, honey. I bet she could. She fixed me a salve that really helped my arthritis. And didn't charge me but a dozen eggs."

Their talk gave Josie an idea. Maybe the conjure woman could fix her up with a brother! That night Josie went to sleep thinking about what she and her new brother were going to do.

At first light Josie slipped out of her house. She gathered a basket of grapes to use as payment. Within the hour she was standing outside the conjure woman's house. A sign said: MADAM ZINNIA—SPELLS, POTIONS, AND SALVES—ALL WELCOME.

What did it look like inside? Josie wondered. Would there be bubbling pots and glowing bottles?

"Come in." A very attractive woman opened the door before Josie could knock. "I've been expecting you," she said, touching the side of Josie's face. "I see you've got a problem? Come, Josie, let Madam Zinnia help you."

Josie was impressed. Madam Zinnia knew her name and even knew she was coming. The girl stepped inside the house and looked around. There were no smoking skulls with cinder-hot eyes. No bats hanging from the ceiling, no bubbling jars of weird-looking stuff. In fact, the living room looked like a picture from a home magazine. It was a sunny room, cheerfully decorated with fresh-cut flowers and interesting whatnots.

Madam Zinnia matched her house in style and disposition. Dressed in a crisp yellow-and-white-checked shirtwaist and white heels, she looked like one of the saleswomen down at Hopperman's Dry Goods Store.

"Come have some fresh-squeezed orange juice and a just-from-the-oven biscuit," the woman said, ushering Josie into the kitchen.

This is all so *normal*, Josie thought.

Madam Zinnia poured two glasses of juice and took a seat at the kitchen table. Josie asked, "Would you please conjure me up a brother? I asked my mother to go to the hospital, but she's still skinny."

"Oh, chile, you can't go round ordering brothers like you do hot dogs at the ballpark."

"I know, but I've waited all summer."

"I see," Madam Zinnia said, giving an understanding nod. "A brother may not be what you really want. I know, because Madam has one. Oh, what a rascal," she said, fanning her face with her pocket handkerchief. "Let Madam conjure you up a fine pet instead."

"My brother will be different."

"Well, a brother you shall have." And closing her eyes tightly, Madam Zinnia said some words Josie didn't know. Then she gave the girl a formula to conjure a brother. "You must do just as I say. Don't change a thing. Find a peach tree twig. Don't strip the leaves. Slide it under your bed from the left side. Then at exactly one minute after midnight, climb into bed from the right side and go to sleep saying whatever name you want to give your brother. Come morning, you'll have a beautiful baby brother."

Josie hurried home and followed the conjure instructions precisely—well, almost. As hard as she tried, she couldn't stay awake until midnight. So she did the conjure spell at ten o'clock instead, and she fell asleep calling her brother's name. "Adam . . . Adam . . . Adam!"

The next morning Josie woke to the smell of country ham and eggs, grits, and biscuits. She rushed into the kitchen. The table was set for four.

"Whose plate is that?" Josie asked, pointing to a place opposite her side of the table.

"Yours," Mama answered, looking at the girl askance.

Josie was surprised, because she'd sat on the right side as long as she'd sat in a chair. "Then whose plate is that?"

"Don't start something with your brother this morning," Mama said, stirring the pot vigorously. "You know very well that's Adam's place."

"My *brother* Adam?" Josie shouted. "It worked, Mama. I conjured up a brother for myself. Isn't it wonderful? Where is he?"

BEWARE!

Mama laughed. "You read too many of those fantasy books, Josie."

But the girl didn't hear. She had bounded out the back door. Mama shrugged and went back to cooking.

Suddenly Josie stopped in her tracks. Something wasn't quite right. Adam was supposed to be a baby. But he was old enough to have a place at the table. Oh, well, she thought. A brother is a brother.

Josie looked behind the garage. "Adam," she called. "Oh, Adam."

All at once someone grabbed her from behind. "You thought you'd catch me off guard. But I gotcha."

Josie tried to turn so she could see her brother, but he held on fast. "Is that you, Adam?" she yelled. "Adam?"

"I won't let you go unless you play In My Power."

"Okay," Josie said, letting him hook his baby finger in hers. "I'm in your power."

Adam let her go immediately. "Okay, who are you? You aren't Josie Hudson. My real sister wouldn't play In My Power without a big fight."

Josie smiled and looked at Adam with wide wondering eyes. He was a shorter version of Daddy, minus a mustache. And though he was frowning at her, the light in his eyes sparkled like sunlight on Mama's chandelier. "But you're my *real* brother," she said. "And we're going to have fun together. I'd love to play In My

Power with you, honest. We'll play whatever you want to play."

Adam backed away humming the *Twilight Zone* theme music. "Earth to Josie. Earth to Josie. Tune in, girl."

Mama called for breakfast, and Adam hurried away. Josie skipped behind, making plans for all the wonderful things she was going to do with her conjure brother.

By the end of the week Josie's joy had turned sour. Nobody seemed to notice that Adam was a conjured brother. It was like he had *always been*. And what made it worse, Adam was the oldest.

Mama and Daddy looked at Adam as if he were something very, very special. He got to ride up front and sit next to Daddy in church. Adam got to cross the pike all by himself and stay up half an hour later at night. How come?

"'Cause I was here first," he teased. Then, snatching the last cookie from the cookie jar, he ran out the door.

"But I didn't ask for an older brother," she complained to Madam Zinnia. "I thought my brother was supposed to be a little baby. What happened?"

The conjure woman stopped weeding her garden, stood, and took off her sunbonnet. "Ahhh, flowers take time and lots of care to grow so pretty," she said, wiping her brow. "Okay, now what's this about the conjure not working? Did you do exactly as I told you?"

Josie looked down at her feet. "Not quite. I couldn't stay awake until midnight, so I did it all at ten o'clock."

BEWARE!

Madam Zinnia shook her head. "Why do people mess with my stuff? That's what happened," she said, snipping roses. "If you had done the conjure at one minute past midnight, the beginning of a new day, you would have gotten a new life, a baby. But you went to sleep at ten, so you got a ten-year-old brother. Sorry, but Madam cannot guarantee a conjure unless it is done properly. I'm afraid you have to live with your big brother."

Josie helped Madam Zinnia plant a beautiful yellow rosebush. "Yellow roses are my favorite," the woman said later, pouring Josie a glass of lemonade. "It takes patience to grow them, lots and lots of patience."

All the next week Josie tried to make the best of a bad situation. No matter what Adam did, Josie went along with it. But the harder she tried, the worse Adam got. "What's wrong with you, silly girl?" he shouted angrily. "You're not acting right. You're so—so stupid!"

"I try to get along with him," Josie told JoBeth at the swings.

"Stop trying so hard," said JoBeth. "Fight back."

So that's what Josie did. That same evening Adam wanted to watch an old movie, but she'd waited all day for her favorite comedy show. She turned the channel, and he pushed her out of the way and flipped it back. Josie fired off a punch to Adam's chin. He hit her back—hard.

"I hate you," she said, wiping away angry tears. "I wish it was just me again."

"Just you," Adam snapped back. "It was great around here until we found you on the railroad tracks and brought you home."

"That's not true!" Josie cried harder. Adam smiled. Daddy broke up the fight and sent them both to bed early with no television. Josie cried herself to sleep.

Arthur Lee and JoBeth came by first thing the next morning.

"We haven't gone over to the pike to watch the big trucks go by in weeks."

"Want to go with us?"

Josie ran to get her bicycle out of the garage. It wasn't there. "Mama, where's my bicycle?"

Mama sighed. "Josie, what are you talking about?" she asked impatiently. "You're the one who made the decision. Adam got the bicycle and you got the chemistry set and the doll dishes."

Josie was shattered. Last Christmas she'd gotten it all—the bicycle, the chemistry set, and the doll dishes.

She rode double on Arthur Lee's bike, feeling awful. The three friends sat on the retaining wall and watched the big wheelers roll past, moving at high speeds. Sometimes the truckers tooted their horns and waved. Usually Josie liked to imitate the sound the trucks made as they passed—"Whoosh! Whoosh!" But she didn't feel like having fun this morning.

"Are big brothers always so awful?" Josie asked.

"Not always," Arthur Lee answered.

"I can't beat Adam up. What should I do?"

BEWARE!

"Get even. That's what I do," said JoBeth.

"Good idea," Josie replied.

Josie put her plan into motion.

Adam had a crush on Lillie, JoBeth's big sister. Josie asked Adam to go with her and JoBeth to the movies. Of course he said no. "JoBeth's big sister is taking her." Adam took the bait—hook, line, and sinker. He agreed to go before he knew it was a horror movie, *Return of the Vampire Mummy*. Adam hated horror movies, but he wouldn't dare admit it. Everything was working perfectly.

At last Saturday came. JoBeth, Lillie, Josie, and Adam met in front of the Ritz. Josie could hardly keep a straight face. During the movie, Josie saw Adam close his eyes when the vampire mummy pushed open the tomb or bit somebody on the neck. And at the end, when the monster shriveled away to dust, Adam slunk down in his seat. Josie knew he was scared to death. Wonderful!

All the kids who lived on Harrison walked home together after the show. It wasn't dark yet, but the sun had set, and lengthy shadows flickered in the last golden light. Josie knew Adam was thinking about vampires that rose at sunset.

As they approached a stretch of vacant property strewn with weeds and trash, Adam moved up to walk with Lillie. Suddenly a caped figure leaped out of nowhere. In the waning light they saw the hideously deformed creature with horrible vampire teeth confronting them.

All eyes were on Adam. The creature reached out to him. He

gasped, his face turned green, and he ran away screaming in terror. Arthur Lee took off his Halloween mask and they all laughed. "He's not so tough and mean now. That'll teach him," said Josie.

But she didn't get the last laugh after all. Adam had gotten home and told his side of the story first. Mama was plenty mad. "What a mean thing to do, Josie Marie Hudson."

"I can't help it if Adam is a scaredy-cat."

"There's nothing wrong with being frightened, but there *is* something wrong with being mean. Embarrassing your brother in front of his friends was unkind and you owe him an apology."

"I won't apologize," Josie said defiantly.

"Don't sass me, girl. What's wrong with you, anyway? For the past few weeks the two of you have been at each other's throats. I've had enough and I want it to stop!"

"I do too," Josie sobbed, and hurried to her room.

Morning came. Josie picked a basket of ripe tomatoes from Mama's garden and went to see Madam Zinnia. "Adam is a conjure brother and I don't want him anymore. Will you give me a spell to make him go away?" she begged, presenting Madam Zinnia with the tomatoes.

"What did that wretched boy do?" Madam Zinnia asked.

"He teases me all the time."

"I have just the thing for a teaser. Madam will put him in a cage and call forth nasty little gremlins to poke at him all day with sticks."

And with a wink she raised her hand. "That will fix him good."

"Stop!" the girl shouted. "He's not that bad. He's just bossy."

"Bossy big brothers! I know about that. Yes, Madam will make him the servant of a terrible beast who lives between the pages of a book." And she raised her hand as if to send him there.

"No." Josie stopped her. "Don't do that. He's not that bossy. He just wants his way all the time."

"Yes. I'll turn him into a big rock sitting in the middle of nowhere. Rocks never get their way about anything."

Josie thought about Adam being a rock. She shook her head.

"No, he's not really so bad. We did have some fun times together. And sometimes I did things to him that weren't so nice either. Oh, I'm all confused."

"I see," said Madam Zinnia, cutting a lovely yellow rose. "Think about it, little one," she said, putting the bloom in the girl's hair, "then tell me, what have you learned from all this?"

"Being the youngest is hard!"

"What a good lesson to learn. I hope you will remember that when you are a big sister . . . one day soon."

"Really? Oh, wow! Wait until I tell Adam."

"But remember," the woman called, "you must be patient."

A sunbeam tickled Josie awake. Mama called her to breakfast, but the kitchen table was only set for three. There was no sign of Adam. He was gone—or had he ever been?

Mama was talking on the telephone. When she hung up, she was smiling. She ran to hug Daddy. "That was the doctor's office. Something wonderful is going to happen," she said. "We're going to have a new baby come January. I hope it will be the brother you've been wanting."

Josie clapped her hands and turned round and round, laughing. "I don't care if it's a boy anymore. Oh, and I'm going to be the best *big sister* in the whole wide world."

"I bet you will," Mama said, laughing too.

Josie was delighted that she was finally getting her wish, but deep down inside she wondered about Adam. Had it all been just a dream? Hopping onto her bicycle, she rode as fast as she could to Madam Zinnia's house.

It was empty and there was a FOR RENT sign in the yard. "Where did Madam Zinnia go?" Josie asked the mailman, who happened to be passing by.

"Madam who? I deliver to a Madam Zonobia, a palm reader over on Lee Avenue. But nobody's lived in this house all summer."

Josie looked at the well-kept flower garden and the lovely yellow rosebush by the side of the house and smiled.

MY SISTER IS A WEREWOLF

by Jack Prelutsky

ILLUSTRATED BY JOE RIVERA

Would that be a problem for you—if your sister was a werewolf?

It's a very *big* problem in this funny poem by Jack Prelutsky.

My Sister
Is a Werewolf

by Jack Prelutsky

My sister is a werewolf.
It's disquieting and strange.
One moonlit night I watched her
Undergo a sudden change.
Her arms and face grew hairy,
And her voice became a roar.
In some ways she looked better
Than she'd ever looked before.

I ran and told our parents,
Who began to fret and fuss
In despair and disapproval,
Moaning, "No! She's not like us!"
I adore my sister dearly
But reluctantly agree—
How I wish she were a vampire
Like her loving family.

THE SURPRISE GUEST

by R.L. Stine

ILLUSTRATED BY MARK FREDRICKSON

Of *course* Halloween is my favorite holiday. I don't need to tell you that, do I? It's the one day of the year when everyone can have good, scary fun.

Over the years, I've read hundreds of creepy Halloween stories. And I've written a few myself. When I sat down to write "The Surprise Guest," I suddenly started to think about ghosts and haunted things. And so I decided to write a ghost story and a Halloween story combined.

The kids in the story think they're throwing a normal Halloween costume party. But they have no idea who is about to show up. . . .

The
Surprise Guest

by R.L. Stine

I had a sleepover at Danny Grover's house the night before Halloween. So I heard the story about the haunted Halloween costume before anyone else.

Danny and I love to tell scary stories. Sometimes we stay up long after midnight, telling story after story, trying to give each other chills.

I tell pretty good ghost stories. But Danny's stories are always more terrifying than mine. He makes up stories like "The Headless Gym Teacher" and "The Werewolf Under the Bed."

The stories are always about people in our families or people we know. Sometimes the stories are so creepy, they make me feel a little cold and shaky.

Danny has a really good imagination.

But this time he swore that the haunted costume story was true.

Beware!

I laughed when he said that.

If only I had believed him. . . .

My name is Tony Wayne. Danny and I are both ten. We've been friends since second grade.

We have a Halloween party every year. Some years it's at my house. This year, it was at Danny's.

Danny's parties are always better than mine. And his costumes are always scarier than mine.

Danny is very popular at school. The girls all think he's the coolest.

I guess it's because he has such a great sense of humor. He is always goofing on things and cracking jokes. He is always breaking up the whole class.

But the teachers all love him anyway. Everyone loves Danny.

He can get away with a lot because of his looks. He has big blue eyes, and curly blond hair, and deep dimples in his cheeks when he flashes that devilish grin.

My seven-year-old sister Claudia thinks that Danny looks like Brad Pitt. She's totally ga-ga over him. When he comes over, she follows him around like a puppy dog.

Why do I hang out with such a total winner? I don't know. I guess maybe I think some of it will rub off on me.

Anyway, the night before the Halloween party, I went over to Danny's house to help out with the decorations.

Danny and I took fat paintbrushes and painted some jack-o-lanterns black. They looked totally creepy. We painted ugly monster faces on some other pumpkins. Danny's were a lot funnier than mine. He's a really good artist.

Danny held one up. "Hey, Tony—this one looks just like Cilla Blakely!" he said.

I burst out laughing.

"That's not funny," Danny's mom said. "Cilla is a lovely girl. Why do you always make fun of her?"

Before we could answer, the doorbell rang.

It was Cilla Blakely. She lives next door. She came over to help Danny get the house ready for the party.

Cilla flipped her long, red hair behind her shoulders. "Hi, Danny. Hey, Tony. What can I do to help?"

"You can climb into the fireplace and see if it works!" Danny joked.

I laughed. But Cilla just groaned and rolled her eyes.

"You can help me with the eyeball punch," Mrs. Grover said. "See? I'm painting Ping-Pong balls to look like eyeballs. Once they're dry we'll drop them in the punch."

"Great!" Cilla said. She picked up a slender paintbrush and began painting eyeballs.

But Danny and I knew the real reason she showed up. She wanted to brag about her costume.

At our parties, we always have a costume contest. Danny and

43

BEWARE!

Cilla always had the two best costumes. But Cilla wins the contest every year.

Last year, Cilla came to the party as a Powerpuff Girl. She had those huge, black eyes. And somehow she had put a thick, black outline around her whole body. She really looked like a cartoon!

Danny just stood there in his ten-foot-tall King Kong costume. He knew that he had lost the contest.

"Go ahead, Cilla," I said. "Tell us what your costume is this year."

"I'm going to be an amazing catwoman," Cilla said. "My costume is awesome." She grinned at Danny. "I don't want to give too much away," she said, "but it's electric. I mean, it's totally wired."

Cilla raked the air with her fingers. She hissed like an angry cat about to attack. "Watch out for my claws, guys!"

"Sounds great," I muttered. I knew my pointy-eared hobbit costume couldn't compete.

"And what second-place costume did you pick out?" Cilla asked Danny.

"I'm not telling," he replied. "My costume this year is so terrifying, I don't want to tell anyone."

Cilla snickered and made a face at him. "You know I always win."

Danny had a strange smile on his face. "Not this year," he whispered. "Not this year."

That night in his room, Danny showed me his costume. A monster costume, covered in orange fur with red and purple scabs up and down the body. The mask was black, an ugly animal face with a wolfish snout open to reveal two rows of jagged yellow fangs.

"What do you think? Is it scary?" Danny asked.

I shook my head. "Pretty good," I said. "But not great." I sighed. "Cilla is going to win again."

Danny hung the costume on a hook on the wall. "You don't know the story of this costume," he whispered. "It *has* to win."

He turned off the lights. We climbed into our beds. And he told me the story in a low, whispery voice.

"This is a true story," he said. "I didn't make it up. The man at the costume store told it to me. He didn't want to sell me the costume."

"Wh-why?" I asked.

"Because the costume may be haunted."

I laughed. "Give me a break," I said.

Danny raised his right hand, as if swearing an oath. "Total truth," he said. "No lie. Just listen. A boy died inside this costume."

I sat up and stared at him. His eyes flashed in the shadowy

light. I could see how excited he was.

Danny continued in a whisper. "This happened a long time ago, at least a hundred years. The boy's name was Henry. He was about our age. He lived in a castle, somewhere in Europe."

"Was he a prince or something?" I asked.

Danny shook his head. "I don't know. I only know he was invited to a fancy costume party at another castle. He wanted to scare everyone at the party. So he had this fur-covered monster costume made. It was created especially for him. But he never made it to the party."

"Why not?" I asked. "How did he die?"

"No one is sure," Danny whispered. "They found him dead on the floor of his room. In front of the mirror. He was wearing the costume. His hands were still gripping the sides of the mask."

I felt a chill run down my back. I stared at the costume.

"Henry was stone-cold dead," Danny continued. "Some people think that he suffocated, that he couldn't get enough air inside the mask.

"But Henry's parents didn't agree. They thought the costume was evil, cursed. They were heartbroken. They didn't want the costume in the castle, but they were afraid to destroy it. They were afraid of its evil. So they stuffed it into a large, wooden trunk and labeled the trunk: NEVER TO BE OPENED. Then they shipped it away on a boat."

"And that's how the costume came to America?" I asked.

BEWARE!

Danny nodded. "The trunk was hidden away for years and years in a big storage warehouse. Then one day about thirty years ago, a boy named James opened the trunk and found it. His father owned the warehouse. His father knew the legend of the costume, but he didn't believe it. So he let James take the costume home."

I swallowed. "Then what happened?" I asked. "What happened to James?"

"James wore it because he wanted to terrify everyone at a Halloween party," Danny said. "Well . . . he did terrify everyone. But not in the way he wanted."

"What do you mean?" I whispered, sitting straight up and hugging myself to stop the shivers.

"James went to the party in the costume, and it was a big success. Kids screamed. Everyone loved it. The costume was so scary. But the scariest moment of all came when James *took off* the costume."

Danny leaned forward, his eyes glowing in the dark bedroom. "You see, at the end of the party, when it came time to take off the costume, James wasn't inside it. A stranger was inside the costume. A surprise guest. A boy no one had ever seen before."

"Huh?" I cried. "You mean—?"

Danny nodded. "Yes," he whispered. "It was Henry. Henry pulled off the costume, stepped up to the startled kids, and introduced himself to everyone."

"But—but—where was James?" I sputtered.

Danny shrugged. "James had disappeared. Gone. Vanished. He was never seen again. Some people think he haunts this costume—just the way Henry did—waiting . . . waiting inside for his chance to come back."

Danny pulled the covers over his chin. "You see?" he whispered. "It's a very scary costume. It has to win tomorrow."

Before the party the next night, I brought my costume over to Danny's. I hung it beside his in the bedroom closet.

Kids were arriving downstairs. Danny rushed out to pick up his cousin Allyson and walk her to the party.

Gazing into the closet, I sighed. My hobbit costume looked pretty lame next to Danny's. I rubbed my hand over the heavy monster fur. I squeezed the hard, yellow fangs on the mask.

And suddenly I had an idea. "I'm going to try on Danny's costume," I murmured.

I'm just going to see what it feels like, I told myself. I lifted the heavy mask between my hands.

Or maybe I'll wear it downstairs. Maybe I'll wear it down to the party and give Danny a little surprise.

After all, why should Danny always get the attention? Why does Danny always have to be the star?

I pulled the monster costume out. I held it up against me and tried to imagine what I would look like inside it.

My heart started to pound. What if Danny's story is true? I

thought. What if the costume really is haunted?

No. That's crazy, I decided. Danny made up that whole story. Danny always makes up scary stories.

I stepped into the furry legs. Then I pulled the costume up over my body. It was much heavier than I'd imagined. And smellier. The fur felt stiff, like the hard bristles on a hairbrush.

I tugged the mask over my head. I twisted it until I could see through the narrow eyeholes.

I started toward the mirror, then suddenly stopped, gripped with fear. Was the costume haunted? Was someone else inside it with me?

I gasped for breath. I felt cold sweat on my forehead.

"James? Are you in here?" I whispered. "James?"

Silence.

My whole body began to itch. My legs felt weak.

"James?"

No. Of *course* there is no one else in here, I told myself. It was another one of Danny's stories.

I tugged the mask off, taking deep breaths of cool air. Then I pulled myself out of the costume. I hung it back up in the closet. And I pulled out the hobbit costume and began to tug it on.

Leaning over, I adjusted the big hobbit feet. Then I pulled on the rubber hobbit mask with its pointy ears. I checked myself out in the mirror. I headed to the stairs.

I stopped on the top step—and a frightened moan escaped my throat. "Ohhhh."

I froze. My costume . . . *I wasn't alone inside it!*

I could sense another presence. I could hear soft breathing.

I could *feel* someone else inside the costume with me.

Trapped inside the dwarflike hobbit body, I felt someone pushing me . . . pushing me out . . . away . . . away.

"Hey—what's going on?" I cried out. My voice sounded muffled and faint. Far away. "Wh-what's happening?"

No answer.

"Is someone there? Answer me! J-James? Is that you?"

"*I've been waiting so long . . .*" a voice whispered. "*And now it's my turn to come out.*"

"No! That's impossible!" I wailed. "You're in *Danny's* costume! He—he told me the whole story. He told me about your ghost—haunting the monster's costume! He—he—"

"*Trick or treat!*" James whispered. "*I switched costumes!*"

And then I could feel him pushing me hard . . . pushing me away . . . into the deep darkness.

I felt weaker . . . weaker . . .

"No—please!" I tried to yell out. But my voice was just a whisper, a distant whisper.

And then I was gone. Outside the costume. All air. No body. I was just air, floating outside the costume.

BEWARE!

And I watched James walk down the stairs. James from thirty years ago. James inside the hobbit costume now.

I could hear him. I could see him. I seemed to float all around him.

Later, at the end of the party, when he pulled off the mask, I saw my horrified friends. And I heard their screams of shock.

I watched them scream. And I heard Cilla shout to the stranger: "Where is Tony? What have you done to Tony?"

She is really worried about me, I realized. Cilla really likes me.

And then I saw Danny clench his hands into tight fists. "Who are you?" he demanded of the stranger. "What are you doing in my house? Where is my friend Tony?"

Good question. Where was I? *Where?*

"My name is James," I heard the boy say. "I am so happy to be at your party."

Yes, James had stepped out of the costume. James was at the party.

But where was I?

I was gone. Floating. Floating in the air.

And then, I felt myself pulled down . . . down . . . into a costume . . . into someone's costume . . . into the deep darkness inside.

That was last year. And now it's almost Halloween once again.

And I'm waiting inside a costume. I'm waiting for my chance to return.

It's been so long. I've been waiting in here so long.

It's my turn. *My* turn.

But who owns the costume? Who plans to wear my costume for Halloween?

Try on *your* costume—okay?

I know it's early. But just try it on. Please?

Please try it on now.

Come on.

What harm could it do?

THE JUDGE'S HOUSE

by Bram Stoker, retold by R.L. Stine

ILLUSTRATED BY VINCE NATALE

You may not know the name Bram Stoker, but you probably will recognize the name of his most famous creation—Dracula.

Stoker's *Dracula* was published over a hundred years ago, in 1897. Thanks to Stoker, we all know the chill of flapping bat wings and the horror of vampire fangs seeking fresh blood.

Collecting stories for this book, I remembered a Bram Stoker story called "The Judge's House." It too was written over one hundred years ago, in a time of horse-drawn carriages and kerosene lamps.

Much of the language was old-fashioned and hard to follow. But the story was still SCARY. So I decided to write my own version, which would be easier for all of us to read and enjoy.

Sorry, no vampires in this story. But I recommend you read it with the lights on . . . especially if you're afraid of RATS!

THE
JUDGE'S HOUSE

by Bram Stoker, retold by R.L. Stine

*Malcolm Malcolmson was warned about
the old judge's house. But he moved in anyway—
and that's when his troubles began. . . .*

Malcolm was a serious young man. Tall and bone thin, he had long, unbrushed brown hair and small, dark brown eyes that always seemed to be squinting because of all the books he read.

One night, his friends found Malcolm packing his suitcase. "My college examination is coming up in three months," he explained. "I want to go somewhere far away, somewhere quiet where I can study in peace."

His friends didn't argue with him. They knew how serious Malcolm was about his studies.

Malcolm packed up all the books he needed. Then he took a train to a tiny town far from his home. He found a quaint inn across from the train station.

Mrs. Witham, the owner, showed him to a small closet of a room. She was a round, red-faced woman with curly, gray hair. She wore a stained white apron over her long, pleated gray dress.

"Have you come to stay for long, young mister?" she asked.

"I need to find a house," Malcolm replied. "A quiet house where I can study without being disturbed."

"This is a quiet town," Mrs. Witham said. "I am sure you will be happy here."

A short while later, Malcolm set out on his search for a place to live. At the edge of town, he discovered an old, rambling house, dark and empty and surrounded by a high brick wall. Malcolm stared at its dust-covered windows, tiny and high above the street.

Even though the sun shone brightly, the house was cloaked in shade.

It looks more like a fort than a house, Malcolm thought. I wonder why no one lives here. He felt a chill. It was as if the sunlight did not dare to touch the house.

This is the place I am looking for, Malcolm decided. No one will bother me here. I can study in complete quiet.

He found the man in charge of the property, who was very happy to rent the house to him. "I am glad to see someone live in the old house," the man told Malcolm. "It has been empty for so long—because of the rumors."

"Rumors?" Malcolm asked.

"Never mind," the man said. He pushed a pen into Malcolm's hand. "Sign here on this line."

Malcolm paid three months' rent. Then he returned to the inn to pick up his belongings. "I have rented the old house on the edge of town," he told Mrs. Witham.

She let out a horrified cry. "Not the judge's house!" Mrs. Witham turned pale.

"Who is the judge?" Malcolm asked.

"He lived there a hundred years ago," the woman explained, trembling. "He was hated by all. He gave the harshest sentences of any judge. No one went free from his courtroom. All who came before him ended in prison forever or faced the hanging rope."

"But what is wrong with his house?" Malcolm asked.

BEWARE!

Mrs. Witham shuddered. "I have heard rumors, sir," she said. "Frightening rumors. There is *something* about that house. If you were my boy, you wouldn't sleep there a night. Not if I had to go there myself and pull the big alarm bell that's on the roof!"

Malcolm laughed. "Don't worry about me," he said. "I'll be studying so hard, I doubt I'll notice any mysterious something."

Exploring the enormous old house, Malcolm trudged through a carpet of dust on the floors. The rooms were bare and dark. The tiny windows near the ceilings didn't let in much light.

He wandered through a maze of long, twisting hallways until he came to the dining room. He gazed at the oak table in the center of the room, the broad, stone fireplace on one wall, the dark paintings that covered the other walls.

This room is much bigger than my apartment back home. It is certainly big enough for all my needs, Malcolm thought. I will make it cozy and warm, and I will live in this room.

To his surprise, he found Mrs. Witham outside. She had brought several men and boys with her. They carried chairs, a new bed, and other items he would need.

Mrs. Witham looked around the big dining room and shivered. "Perhaps, sir, since the room is big and drafty, you might put a tall wooden screen around your bed at night."

Malcolm laughed. "And what will a screen keep out?"

"Rats and mice and beetles," Mrs. Witham replied. "Do you

think that these old walls are not home to many a rat?"

"I'm not afraid of a few rats," Malcolm said. "I'll be studying so hard, I won't even hear them."

If only he had listened to the kind woman's warnings. . . .

Later that day, Malcolm hired an old woman named Mrs. Dempster to look after him. Then he took a long walk, studying a book as he strolled.

When he returned in the evening, he found the room swept and tidied, a fire burning in the hearth, the lamp lit. The table was spread for supper with Mrs. Dempster's excellent food.

"This is comfort indeed," Malcolm said, rubbing his hands in the fire's warmth.

After eating his fill, Malcolm moved the food away and placed his books on the table. Listening to the pleasant crackle of the fire, he began to study.

Malcolm read for several hours until his eyes grew tired. He shut them for a moment but opened them quickly. "What is that sound?"

Not the crackle of the fire. But a scraping, clawing sound. As if something were scratching to get into the room.

No, wait. He heard hard thumps. More scratching. At the ceiling? Under the floor? From behind the big paintings on the walls?

He held his breath and listened.

BEWARE!

Scratch . . . scratch . . .

Thumpthumpthump . . .

Mrs. Witham was right. The house was filled with rats!

Dozens of them? Hundreds?

Malcolm could hear them, above the ceiling and under the floor and behind the paintings on the walls! Racing and gnawing and scratching!

Malcolm swallowed hard. He took a deep breath.

Then he clapped his hands over his ears and bent over his book. "Shut them out. Shut them out," he muttered. He tried to return to his studies.

But the scratching sounds echoed in his ears. He took his lamp and walked around the big room, exploring. He could hear the rats scampering everywhere. But they stayed out of sight.

He stopped to gaze at the old pictures that covered the walls. They were coated so thickly with dust and dirt, he couldn't make out any details.

He stepped closer to the wall of paintings—then froze in fear. His hands began to tremble and he almost dropped the lamp.

The walls were filled with cracks and holes. And from every crack and hole, eyes stared out at him. Hundreds of rats' eyes. Bright eyes glittering in the lamplight. Bright, shiny eyes staring at him from all around the room.

Keep calm, Malcolm told himself. Keep calm. They will not attack. They are too frightened to come out in the open.

He crossed the room and gazed at the rope of the great alarm bell on the roof. It hung down into the room on the right side of the fireplace.

Malcolm returned to the table. He forced himself to study again. For a while, the rats disturbed him with their racing and scratching. But soon he became so drawn into his book, he didn't hear the sounds.

Late at night, he finally looked up from his reading. The fire had fallen low but still threw out a deep, red glow. The room was strangely quiet.

As Malcolm's gaze wandered—he gasped. On the back of the tall oak chair by the fireplace stood a creature. An enormous rat. It glared at him with red, angry eyes.

It's as big as a cat! Malcolm's heart began to pound. *What has it been feeding on to make it grow so big?*

He stared back at the rat. Stared at the creature's glowing eyes. Human eyes, he thought. Not the eyes of a rodent.

"GO!" Malcolm screamed at the top of his voice. "GO AWAY!"

The fat rodent didn't budge.

Malcolm swung his arm hard at the creature, as if batting it away. Then he pretended to throw something at it. Again, the rat didn't stir, but it hissed and showed its sharp, white teeth.

Malcolm jumped up from the table. He grabbed the fireplace poker and ran at the rat. The rat let out another angry hiss. Then it leaped from the chair, darted across the floor, and raced up the rope of the alarm bell. In seconds, it disappeared into the darkness above.

Breathing hard, Malcolm stood with the poker in his hand, staring up at the dark, empty ceiling. Weariness swept over him. I must get some sleep, he thought. Plenty of time to worry about rats tomorrow. . . .

The next morning, Malcolm felt tired after his long night of studying. But a strong cup of tea helped to wake him up.

He found a quiet path between high elm trees that led out of town. He walked most of the day, reading his book along the way.

When he returned to town, he ran into Mrs. Witham, the innkeeper. "You must not overdo it, sir," she scolded. "You are paler this morning than you should be. Tell me, how did your first night go?"

"Not bad," Malcolm replied. "Except for the rats. You were right, Mrs. Witham. The house is infested with them. There was one wicked-looking old devil that sat on my chair by the fire. He wouldn't go until I took a poker to him."

"Mercy on us!" Mrs. Witham exclaimed. "An old devil, sitting on a chair by the fireside. Take care, sir. Take care."

That night, the scampering of the rats began earlier. They scurried up and down, under and over. They squeaked and scratched and gnawed.

Malcolm's breath caught in his throat as they poked their heads out of the chinks and cracks in the walls. Their eyes shone like tiny lamps as the firelight rose and fell.

They sprang out from the holes. They climbed onto the tops of the big paintings. Then, snapping their tails, they formed a circle around the room.

Malcolm felt chill after chill run down his back. They are getting bolder, he thought. They are getting braver.

He banged the table with his fist, trying to scare them away.

He tried to concentrate on his studies. He covered his ears with his hands as he leaned over his book.

All at once, the rat sounds stopped. Malcolm sat up, alert and surprised.

Silence. The silence of the grave, he thought.

The rats had all vanished.

What made them disappear?

He raised his eyes to the chair by the fire—and gasped.

There on the high-backed chair sat the enormous rat. Once again, the rat glared at him coldly with blood-red eyes.

The others disappear when this rat arrives, Malcolm thought. Are they frightened of it?

The huge rat bared its teeth and hissed at Malcolm.

Malcolm picked up his heavy textbook and flung it at the fat, gray creature. His aim was poor. The book hit the wall and dropped to the floor. The rat didn't stir.

BEWARE!

With an angry cry, Malcolm raced across the room, grabbed the fireplace poker, and came at the rat, swinging the poker in front of him.

Once again, the rat uttered an angry hiss. Its red eyes burned with hatred.

Malcolm swung the heavy poker. The rat dropped heavily off the chair. It scampered up the alarm bell rope and pulled itself out of sight.

Where does it go up there? Malcolm wondered. Is there a hole in the ceiling where it escapes?

Malcolm couldn't see that high. His kerosene lamp was too dim, and the fire had burned low.

Malcolm stared at the large paintings high on the wall. He couldn't see them, either. I must have them cleaned, he decided. And I must burn more lamps in this room.

He pulled his watch from his trouser pocket. Nearly midnight. He threw some logs on the fire, then made a pot of tea.

While he sipped his tea, he thought about the giant rat. He shuddered. That rat is too bold, he thought. Is it challenging me by sitting up like a human in the chair? Is it planning to attack?

If I could find out where it escapes, perhaps I could set a trap for it.

Once again, the rats began to scamper above his head and beneath the floor. Malcolm searched the house until he found another lamp. He lit it and placed it on the fireplace mantel.

That's better, he thought. I can see a little better.

He returned to the table and piled up all of the books he had brought with him. I want them handy so I can throw them at the ugly creature, he thought.

Then Malcolm lifted the rope of the alarm bell and placed the end of it on the table. He tucked the end under the burning table lamp.

"There now, my friend," Malcolm said. "If you start to climb down the rope, the lamp will shake. I will know you are coming. And I will be ready for you."

The rats clawed and scratched the walls. Malcolm couldn't see them. But he could hear them chewing. Hear the thud of their feet over his head. Hear the scrape and slap of their tails over the wood.

"GO AWAY! GO AWAY!" he wailed.

But the rats ignored his shouts and continued their ugly noises.

Clamping his hands over his ears, Malcolm returned to his studies. He worked long into the night—until he realized the house had grown silent again.

A deep silence. The only sound Malcolm could hear was the beating of his heart.

And then . . . the rope jiggled.

The lamp moved.

BEWARE!

Malcolm looked up in time to see the enormous rat drop from the rope onto the armchair. It sat there, glaring at him.

Malcolm raised a book. He took careful aim. He flung it at the rat.

The rat sprang aside. The book flew past it.

Malcolm grabbed another book, and another, and another. He threw them at the rat, but the big creature dodged each one.

Breathing hard, Malcolm grabbed one last book. He raised it high and aimed. To his surprise, the rat squeaked and whimpered and seemed afraid.

Malcolm heaved the book—and it struck the rat.

"EEEEEEE!" The rat uttered a horrifying shriek. It made a great jump for the rope and pulled itself up as fast as it could.

By the light of the new lamp, Malcolm could see where the rat had escaped. It leaped to a molding on the wall—then disappeared through a hole in one of the large, dust-covered paintings.

"The third painting from the fireplace," Malcolm said. "I shall not forget. Tomorrow I shall find my fat friend's home and set a trap up there. That rat shall pay me no more visits."

Malcolm bent to pick up the book that had hit the rat—and let out a gasp. "The Bible my mother gave me! What an odd coincidence. . . ."

The next morning, Malcolm gave Mrs. Dempster special instructions. "Please find a ladder and wash those paintings—especially the third one from the fireplace. I want to see what they are."

Malcolm studied his books all day in the shaded walk outside of town. In the afternoon, he paid a visit to Mrs. Witham at her inn. She introduced him to a man named Dr. Thornhill.

"Mrs. Witham asked me to speak to you," the doctor said.

He was a white-haired man with a short, snowy beard. He had a round, red face and a bulging stomach under his black suit jacket. "She doesn't like the idea of your being in that house by yourself."

"I am not afraid of the house," Malcolm replied. "But I am having a problem with the rats—one big creature in particular."

He told Dr. Thornhill about his adventures with the giant rat. Mrs. Witham sighed and shook her head.

Dr. Thornhill's face grew grim. "The rat always disappears up the rope of the alarm bell?" he asked.

"Always," Malcolm replied.

The doctor rubbed his beard and was silent for a long moment. Then he said, "I suppose you know what the rope is?"

Malcolm shook his head no.

"It is the hanging rope that the judge used on his victims," Dr. Thornhill said.

Malcolm thought about the doctor's words as he walked home. He seemed like a kindly man, Malcolm thought. Why did he tell me about that rope? Was he trying to frighten me or help me?

BEWARE!

Dr. Thornhill had given Malcolm instructions. "If you have any kind of fright tonight, ring the alarm bell. If I hear the bell, I will hurry to your rescue."

Rescue? Malcolm thought.

Why would I need to be rescued?

Malcolm returned home to find the place bright and tidy, with a cheerful fire and the lamps glowing. The night was cold for April. A heavy wind blew. Raindrops began to patter against the windows.

Malcolm ate his dinner and settled down to work. But he couldn't concentrate.

Once again, he heard the claw and scrape of the rats, even over the sounds of the storm. A million tiny eyes peered out at him from every crack and hole in the wall.

Why are you watching me? Malcolm wondered. Are you *expecting* something to happen tonight?

The rope suddenly rose and fell.

Malcolm uttered a cry.

Then he realized it was caused by the storm winds blowing hard against the alarm bell on the roof.

"*It is the hanging rope that the judge used on his victims.*" Dr. Thornhill's solemn words came back to Malcolm.

Malcolm felt a shiver roll down the back of his neck. Lifting the lamp, he crossed the room to the paintings on the wall. They had been dusted and washed. And now he could see them clearly.

He raised the lamp to the third painting from the fire—and felt another shiver.

It was of a judge dressed in a scarlet robe. The face was strong and evil, with a beaklike nose and cold, glowing eyes.

The eyes . . .

Malcolm stared at the judge's face with growing horror.

The eyes . . .

"No! It cannot be!" Malcolm cried.

The eyes . . . they were the same as the rat's eyes!

Malcolm's heart began to thud in his chest. He suddenly felt cold all over.

He gazed hard at the painting. The judge was seated in a high-backed oak chair. The chair stood to the right of a wide stone fireplace. Behind it, a rope hung down from the ceiling.

"It is *this* room," Malcolm whispered. "It is *this room* in the painting."

His whole body shook. He spun around.

And a cry escaped his throat.

There, in the judge's chair, with the rope hanging behind, sat the rat.

It stared hard at Malcolm with cold, dark eyes . . . the same eyes . . . the same eyes as the judge in the painting. . . .

The lamp fell from Malcolm's hand. Oil spilled over the

floor. His body trembling, he bent to pick up the lamp.

When he turned back to the chair, the rat was gone.

The rope swayed. Malcolm saw the big rat scurrying up the rope.

Then halfway up the rope, it stopped. It lowered its head and furiously began to gnaw.

What is it doing? Malcolm wondered. Why is it chewing at the rope?

Outside, the wind howled. Waves of rain battered the windows.

Malcolm stared up helplessly as the rat chewed through the rope. After a few seconds, a long section of rope fell to the floor in front of the chair.

The rat clung to the remaining rope.

Dr. Thornhill's words came back to him: "*If you have any kind of fright tonight, ring the alarm bell. I will hurry to your rescue.*"

But I can't reach it now, Malcolm realized. Now I can't pull the rope to call for help!

And then Malcolm let out a shrill cry of horror as his eyes returned to the third painting on the wall.

How could that be? How?

A wide brown patch filled the center of the painting.

The judge had disappeared from the painting.

Malcolm spun around, and in a chill of horror, he saw the judge. Saw the judge in his scarlet robe, sitting on the oak chair.

He wore a cold smile of triumph on his face. And as his smile grew wider, the clock began to chime.

Midnight.

Slowly, the judge rose from the chair. As Malcolm stared in fright, the judge picked up the piece of rope. He drew it through his hands, smiling all the while. Then he began to knot one end of it, tying it into a noose.

Holding the rope in both hands, the judge moved in front of the door.

I'm trapped, Malcolm realized. He has me trapped here.

The judge moved closer, staying between Malcolm and the door. He raised the noose—and threw it at Malcolm.

Malcolm tried to dodge away. But his legs were trembling too hard to move.

The loop of the rope narrowly missed him.

His eyes glowing, the judge raised the noose again—and tossed it at Malcolm.

Malcolm uttered a faint cry.

Another near miss.

Malcolm's heart pounded. He searched the room, frantically looking for a way to escape. To his horror, the rats began to come out of their holes.

Hundreds of them huddled around the walls, red eyes glowing. Snapping their jaws, whipping their tails, chittering and shrieking, they moved in, tightening their circle.

BEWARE!

More rats poured out from behind the painting. They swarmed over the mantel, over the table. Rats covered every surface.

Glancing up, Malcolm saw the rope to the alarm bell covered with rats. Every inch. And still more and more rats poured out from the ceiling onto the rope.

The rope grew heavier. Heavier. And the bell began to ring.

Yes! Malcolm thought. The rats are ringing the alarm!

The bell rang louder. And louder.

Yes! Malcolm thought. Ring the alarm. Ring the alarm to bring help!

The bell clanged. The rats began to squeal. The wind howled.

The judge stepped up and lowered the rope around Malcolm's neck.

The people of the village heard the clang of the alarm bell. A crowd came running through the storm with lamps and torches.

Dr. Thornhill was the first to arrive. He pounded on the door, but there was no reply. "Break down the door! Hurry!" he boomed.

The men used a wide tree branch to break it down. Dr. Thornhill rushed into the dining room. The villagers followed close behind him.

74

"Nooooo!" He moaned as he saw Malcolm's body swinging from the end of the alarm bell rope.

And then he turned in horror and saw the face of the judge in the painting. The judge's face with its broad, triumphant smile.

THE CREMATION OF SAM McGEE

by Robert W. Service

ILLUSTRATED BY JACK DAVIS

When I was a kid, I loved listening to stories on the radio. Stories I heard on the radio were so much more exciting than on TV— because I had to picture them in my own imagination.

A radio storyteller named Jean Shepherd introduced me to Robert W. Service. Shepherd had an all-night radio show that started at midnight. As a kid, I would sneak my radio into my bed and stay up most of the night with the radio pressed to my ear, listening to his stories.

Sometimes Shepherd read Robert Service's poems. They weren't like any poems I had ever heard before. They were about hard, dangerous men out in a cold, unfriendly world. The poems were tough. They made you shiver. They made your blood run cold.

If you think poems can't give you a chill, try this one. It's my all-time favorite.

THE CREMATION
OF SAM McGEE

by Robert W. Service

There are strange things done in the midnight sun
By the men who moil for gold;
The Arctic trails have their secret tales
That would make your blood run cold;
The Northern Lights have seen queer sights,
But the queerest they ever did see
Was that night on the marge of Lake Lebarge
I cremated Sam McGee.

BEWARE!

Now Sam McGee was from Tennessee,
   where the cotton blooms and blows.
Why he left his home in the South to roam
   'round the Pole, God only knows.
He was always cold, but the land of gold
   seemed to hold him like a spell;
Though he'd often say in his homely way
   that "he'd sooner live in hell."

On a Christmas Day we were mushing our way
   over the Dawson trail.
Talk of your cold! through the parka's fold
   it stabbed like a driven nail.
If our eyes we'd close, then the lashes froze
   till sometimes we couldn't see;
It wasn't much fun, but the only one
   to whimper was Sam McGee.

And that very night, as we lay packed tight
   in our robes beneath the snow,
And the dogs were fed, and the stars o'erhead
   were dancing heel and toe,
He turned to me, and "Cap," says he,
   "I'll cash in this trip, I guess;
And if I do, I'm asking that you
   won't refuse my last request."

Well, he seemed so low that I couldn't say no;
 then he says with a sort of moan:
"It's the cursed cold, and it's got right hold
 till I'm chilled clean through to the bone.
Yet 'tain't being dead—it's my awful dread
 of the icy grave that pains;
So I want you to swear that, foul or fair,
 you'll cremate my last remains."

A pal's last need is a thing to heed,
 so I swore I would not fail;
And we started on at the streak of dawn;
 but God! he looked ghastly pale.
He crouched on the sleigh, and he raved all day
 of his home in Tennessee;
And before nightfall a corpse was all
 that was left of Sam McGee.

There wasn't a breath in that land of death,
 and I hurried, horror-driven,
With a corpse half hid that I couldn't get rid,
 because of a promise given;
It was lashed to the sleigh, and it seemed to say:
 "You may tax your brawn and brains,
But you promised true, and it's up to you
 to cremate those last remains."

BEWARE!

Now a promise made is a debt unpaid,
    and the trail has its own stern code.
In the days to come, though my lips were dumb,
    in my heart how I cursed that load.
In the long, long night, by the lone firelight,
    while the huskies, round in a ring,
Howled out their woes to the homeless snows
    —O God! how I loathed the thing.

And every day that quiet clay seemed to heavy
    and heavier grow;
And on I went, though the dogs were spent
    and the grub was getting low;
The trail was bad, and I felt half mad,
    but I swore I would not give in;
And I'd often sing to the hateful thing,
    and it hearkened with a grin.

Till I came to the marge of Lake Lebarge,
    and a derelict there lay;
It was jammed in the ice, but I saw in a trice
    it was called the "Alice May."
And I looked at it, and I thought a bit,
    and I looked at my frozen chum;
Then "Here," said I, with a sudden cry,
    "is my cre-ma-tor-eum."

Some planks I tore from the cabin floor,
and I lit the boiler fire;
Some coal I found that was lying around,
and I heaped the fuel higher;
The flames just soared, and the furnace roared
—such a blaze you seldom see;
And I burrowed a hole in the glowing coal,
and I stuffed in Sam McGee.

BEWARE!

Then I made a hike, for I didn't like
  to hear him sizzle so;
And the heavens scowled, and the huskies howled,
  and the wind began to blow.
It was icy cold, but the hot sweat rolled
  down my cheeks, and I don't know why;
And the greasy smoke in an inky cloak
  went streaking down the sky.

I do not know how long in the snow
  I wrestled with grisly fear;
But the stars came out and they danced about
  ere again I ventured near;
I was sick with dread, but I bravely said:
  "I'll just take a peep inside.
I guess he's cooked, and it's time I looked";
  . . . then the door I opened wide.

And there sat Sam, looking cool and calm,
  in the heart of the furnace roar;
And he wore a smile you could see a mile,
  and he said: "Please close that door.
It's fine in here, but I greatly fear
  you'll let in the cold and storm—
Since I left Plumtree, down in Tennessee,
  it's the first time I've been warm."

There are strange things done in the midnight sun
By the men who moil for gold;
The Arctic trails have their secret tales
That would make your blood run cold;
The Northern Lights have seen queer sights,
But the queerest they ever did see
Was that night on the marge of Lake Lebarge
I cremated Sam McGee.

The Elevator

by *William Sleator*

ILLUSTRATED BY PATRICK ARRASMITH

I live in New York City, so I ride in a *lot* of elevators. I'm not afraid of them, but sometimes they give me creepy thoughts.

For example: What if every time you stepped into an elevator the same person was there? At first, it would be kind of funny. You'd think it a strange coincidence. But by the third or fourth time, you'd start to think something weird was going on. Is this person following you?

William Sleator is one of my favorite authors. He has a great ability to make ordinary situations absolutely terrifying. And he can make truly bizarre and terrifying situations believable.

William Sleator must have the same feeling about elevators that I do—since he wrote this truly frightening story.

Most elevators go up and down. But this elevator is a one-way ride to terror!

THE ELEVATOR

by William Sleator

It was an old building with an old elevator—a very small elevator, with a maximum capacity of three people. Martin, a thin twelve-year-old, felt nervous in it from the first day he and his father moved into the apartment. Of course he was always uncomfortable in elevators, afraid that they would fall, but there was something especially unpleasant about this one. Perhaps its baleful atmosphere was due to the light from the single fluorescent ceiling strip, bleak and dim on the dirty brown walls. Perhaps the problem was the door, which never stayed open quite long enough, and slammed shut with such ominous, clanging finality. Perhaps it was the way the mechanism shuddered in a kind of exhaustion each time it left a floor, as though it might never reach the next one. Maybe it was simply the dimensions of the contraption that bothered him, so small that it felt uncomfortably crowded even when there was only one other person in it.

Coming home from school the day after they moved in, Martin tried the stairs. But they were almost as bad, windowless, shadowy, with several dark landings where the light bulbs had burned out. His footsteps echoed behind him like slaps on the cement, as though there was another person climbing, getting closer. By the time he reached the seventeenth floor, which seemed to take forever, he was winded and gasping.

His father, who worked at home, wanted to know why he was so out of breath. "But why didn't you take the elevator?" he asked, frowning at Martin when he explained about the stairs. Not only are you skinny and weak and bad at sports, his expression seemed to say, but you're also a coward. After that, Martin forced himself to take the elevator. He would have to get used to it, he told himself, just the way he got used to being bullied at school, and always picked last when they chose teams. The elevator was an undeniable fact of life.

He didn't get used to it. He remained tense in the trembling little box, his eyes fixed on the numbers over the door that blinked on and off so haltingly, as if at any moment they might simply give up. Sometimes he forced himself to look away from them, to the Emergency Stop button, or the red Alarm button. What would happen if he pushed one of them? Would a bell ring? Would the elevator stop between floors? And if it did, how would they get him out?

That was what he hated about being alone on the thing—the fear of being trapped there for hours by himself. But it wasn't much better when there were other passengers. He felt too close to any other rider, too intimate. And he was always very conscious of the effort people made not to look at one another, staring fixedly at nothing. Being short, in this one situation, was an advantage, since his face was below the eye level of adults, and after a brief glance they ignored him.

Until the morning the elevator stopped at the fourteenth floor, and the fat lady got on. She wore a threadbare green coat that ballooned around her; her ankles bulged above dirty sneakers. As she waddled into the elevator, Martin was sure he felt it sink under her weight. She was so big that she filled the cubicle; her coat brushed against him, and he had to squeeze into the corner to make room for her—there certainly wouldn't have been room for another passenger. The door slammed quickly behind her. And then, unlike everyone else, she did not stand facing the door. She stood with her back to the door, wheezing, staring directly at Martin.

For a moment he met her gaze. Her features seemed very small, squashed together by the loose, fleshy mounds of her

cheeks. She had no chin, only a great swollen mass of neck, barely contained by the collar of her coat. Her sparse red hair was pinned back by a plastic barrette. And her blue eyes, though tiny, were sharp and penetrating, boring into Martin's face.

Abruptly he looked away from her to the numbers over the door. She didn't turn around. Was she still looking at him? His eyes slipped back to hers, then quickly away. She was still watching him. He wanted to close his eyes; he wanted to turn around and stare into the corner, but how could he? The elevator creaked down to twelve, down to eleven. Martin looked at his watch; he looked at the numbers again. They weren't even down to nine yet. And then, against his will, his eyes slipped back to her face. She was still watching him. Her nose tilted up; there was a large space between her nostrils and her upper lip, giving her a piggish look. He looked away again, clenching his teeth, fighting the impulse to squeeze his eyes shut against her.

She had to be crazy. Why else would she stare at him this way? What was she going to do next?

She did nothing. She only watched him, breathing audibly, until the elevator reached the first floor at last. Martin would have rushed past her to get out, but there was no room. He could only wait as she turned—reluctantly, it seemed to him—and moved so slowly out into the lobby. And then he ran. He didn't care what she thought. He ran past her, outside into the fresh air, and he ran almost all the way to school. He had never felt such relief in his life.

He thought about her all day. Did she live in the building? He had never seen her before, and the building wasn't very big— only four apartments on each floor. It seemed likely that she didn't live there, and had only been visiting somebody.

But if she were only visiting somebody, why was she leaving the building at seven thirty in the morning? People didn't make visits at that time of day. Did that mean she *did* live in the building? If so, it was likely—it was a certainty—that sometime he would be riding with her on the elevator again.

He was apprehensive as he approached the building after school. In the lobby, he considered the stairs. But that was ridiculous. Why should he be afraid of an old lady? If he was afraid of her, if he let it control him, then he was worse than all the names they called him at school. He pressed the button; he stepped into the empty elevator. He stared at the lights, urging the elevator on. It stopped on three.

At least it's not fourteen, he told himself; the person she was visiting lives on fourteen. He watched the door slide open— revealing a green coat, a piggish face, blue eyes already fixed on him as though she knew he'd be there.

It wasn't possible. It was like a nightmare. But there she was, massively real. "Going up!" he said, his voice a humiliating squeak.

She nodded, her flesh quivering, and stepped on. The door slammed. He watched her pudgy hand move toward the buttons. She pressed, not fourteen, but eighteen, the top floor, one floor above his own. The elevator trembled and began its ascent. The fat lady watched him.

He knew she had gotten on at fourteen this morning. So why was she on three, going up to eighteen now? The only floors *he* ever went to were seventeen and one. What was she doing? Had she been waiting for him? Was she riding with him on purpose?

But that was crazy. Maybe she had lots of friends in the building. Or else she was a cleaning lady who worked in different apartments. That had to be it. He felt her eyes on him as he stared at the numbers slowly blinking on and off—slower than usual, it seemed to him. Maybe the elevator was having trouble because of how heavy she was. It was supposed to carry three adults, but it was old. What if it got stuck between floors? What if it fell?

They were on five now. It occurred to him to press seven, get off there, and walk the rest of the way. And he would have done it, if he could have reached the buttons. But there was no room to get past her without squeezing against her, and he could not bear the thought of any physical contact with her. He concentrated on being in his room. He would be home soon, only another minute or so. He could stand anything for a minute, even this crazy lady watching him.

Unless the elevator got stuck between floors. Then what would he do? He tried to push the thought away, but it kept coming back. He looked at her. She was still staring at him, no expression at all on her squashed little features.

When the elevator stopped on his floor, she barely moved out of the way. He had to inch past her, rubbing against her horrible scratchy coat, terrified the door would close before he made it through. She quickly turned and watched him as the door slammed shut. And he thought, *Now she knows I live on seventeen.*

"Did you ever notice a strange fat lady on the elevator?" he asked his father that evening.

"Can't say as I have," he said, not looking away from the television.

He knew he was probably making a mistake, but he had to tell somebody. "Well, she was on the elevator with me twice today. And the funny thing was, she just kept staring at me, she never stopped looking at me for a minute. You think . . . you know of anybody who has a weird cleaning lady or anything?"

"What are you so worked up about now?" his father said,

turning impatiently away from the television.

"I'm not worked up. It was just funny the way she kept staring at me. You know how people never look at each other in the elevator. Well, she just kept looking at me."

"What am I going to do with you, Martin?" his father said. He sighed and shook his head. "Honestly, now you're afraid of some poor old lady."

"I'm not afraid."

"You're afraid," said his father, with total assurance. "When are you going to grow up and act like a man? Are you going to be timid all your life?"

He managed not to cry until he got to his room—but his father probably knew he was crying anyway. He slept very little.

And in the morning, when the elevator door opened, the fat lady was waiting for him.

She was expecting him. She knew he lived on seventeen. He stood there, unable to move, and then backed away. And as he did so, her expression changed. She smiled as the door slammed.

He ran for the stairs. Luckily, the unlit flight on which he fell was between sixteen and fifteen. He only had to drag himself up one and a half flights with the terrible pain in his leg. His father was silent on the way to the hospital, disappointed and annoyed at him for being such a coward and a fool.

BEWARE!

It was a simple fracture. He didn't need a wheelchair, only a cast and crutches. But he was condemned to the elevator now. Was that why the fat lady had smiled? Had she known it would happen this way?

At least his father was with him on the elevator on the way back from the hospital. There was no room for the fat lady to get on. And even if she did, his father would see her, he would realize how peculiar she was, and then maybe he would understand. And once they got home, he could stay in the apartment for a few days—the doctor had said he should use the leg as little as possible. A week, maybe—a whole week without going on the elevator. Riding up with his father, leaning on his crutches, he looked around the little cubicle and felt a kind of triumph. He had beaten the elevator, and the fat lady, for the time being. And the end of the week was very far away.

"Oh, I almost forgot," his father reached out his hand and pressed nine.

"What are you doing? You're not getting off, are you?" he asked him, trying not to sound panicky.

"I promised Terry Ullman I'd drop in on her," his father said, looking at his watch as he stepped off.

"Let me go with you. I want to visit her, too," Martin pleaded, struggling forward on his crutches.

But the door was already closing. "Afraid to be on the elevator alone?" his father said, with a look of total scorn. "Grow up, Martin." The door slammed shut.

Martin hobbled to the buttons and pressed nine, but it didn't do any good. The elevator stopped at ten, where the fat lady was waiting for him. She moved in quickly; he was too slow, too unsteady on his crutches to work his way past her in time. The door sealed them in; the elevator started up.

"Hello, Martin," she said, and laughed, and pushed the Stop button.

THE WITCHES

by Roald Dahl

ILLUSTRATED BY QUENTIN BLAKE

Y ou are trapped in a room filled with two hundred witches. Witches who remove their faces to reveal their shrunken, shriveled, crumpled, rotting faces beneath. Witches who are dedicated to Cruelty for Children.

Frightening? Funny? Time to open your mouth and scream?

Yes.

People of all ages love Roald Dahl's delightfully devilish creations. I read his adult stories before I discovered his children's books, and I loved them. Dahl has such a wicked view of the world. In his stories, quiet, normal people often turn out to be evil in the most surprising ways.

But I like his children's stories even better. Here is one of my favorite, frightful scenes from *The Witches*. Watch out! The Grand High Witch is about to enter now. . . .

THE WITCHES

by Roald Dahl

THE MEETING

Now that the Manager had gone, I was not particularly alarmed. What better than to be imprisoned in a room full of these splendid ladies. If I ever got talking to them, I might even suggest that they come and do a bit of cruelty-to-children-preventing at my school. We could certainly use them there.

In they came, talking their heads off as women always do when you get a whole bunch of them together. They began milling around and choosing their seats, and there was a whole lot of stuff like, "Come and sit next to me, Millie dear," and "Oh, hel-*lo*, Beatrice! I haven't seen you since the last meeting! What an adorable dress you have on!"

BEWARE!

I decided to stay where I was and let them get on with their meeting while I got on with my mouse training, but I watched them for a while longer through the crack in the screen, waiting for them to settle down. How many were there? I guessed about two hundred. The back rows filled up first. They all seemed to want to sit as far back from the platform as possible.

In the middle of the back row there was a lady wearing a tiny green hat who kept scratching the nape of her neck. She couldn't leave it alone. It fascinated me the way her fingers kept scratching away at the hair on the back of her neck. Had she known somebody was watching her from behind, I'm sure she would have been embarrassed. I wondered if she had dandruff. All of a sudden I noticed that the lady next to her was doing the same thing!

And the next one!

And the next!

The whole lot of them were doing it. They were all scratching away like mad at the hair on the backs of their necks!

Did they have fleas in their hair?

More likely it was nits.

A boy at school called Ashton had had nits in his hair last term and the matron had made him dip his whole head in turpentine. It killed the nits all right, but it nearly killed Ashton as well. Half the skin came way from his scalp.

I began to be fascinated by these hair-scratching ladies. It is always funny when you catch someone doing something coarse and she thinks no one is looking. Nose picking, for example, or scratching her bottom. Hair scratching is very nearly as unattractive, especially if it goes on and on.

I decided it had to be nits.

Then the most astonishing thing happened. I saw one lady pushing her fingers up *underneath* the hair on her head, and the hair, *the entire head of hair*, lifted upward all in one piece, and the hand slid underneath the hair and went on scratching!

She was wearing a wig! She was also wearing gloves! I glanced swiftly around at the rest of the now seated audience. *Every one of them was wearing gloves!*

My blood turned to ice. I began to shake all over. I glanced frantically behind me for a back door to escape through. There wasn't one.

Should I leap out from behind the screen and make a dash for the double doors?

Those double doors were already closed and I could see a woman standing in front of them. She was bending forward and fixing some sort of a metal chain around the two door handles.

Keep still, I told myself. No one has seen you yet. There's no reason in the world why they should come and look behind the screen. But one false move, one cough, one sneeze, one nose blow, one little sound of any sort, and it won't be just one witch that gets

BEWARE!

you. It'll be two hundred!

At that point, I think I fainted. The whole thing was altogether too much for a small boy to cope with. But I don't believe I was out for more than a few seconds, and when I came to, I was lying on the carpet and I was still, thank heavens, behind the screen. There was absolute silence all around me.

Rather shakily, I got to my knees and peered once again through the crack in the screen.

FRiZZLED LiKE A FRiTTER

All the women, or rather the witches, were now sitting motionless in their chairs and staring as though hypnotized at somebody who had suddenly appeared on the platform. That somebody was another woman.

The first thing I noticed about this woman was her size. She was tiny, probably no more than four and a half feet tall. She looked quite young, I guessed about twenty-five or -six, and she was very pretty. She had on a rather stylish long black dress that reached almost to the ground and she wore black gloves that came up to her elbows. Unlike the others, she wasn't wearing a hat.

She didn't look to me like a witch at all, but she couldn't possibly *not* be one, otherwise what on earth was she doing up there on the platform? And why, for heaven's sake, were all the other witches gazing at her with such a mixture of adoration, awe, and fear?

Very slowly, the young lady on the platform raised her hands to her face. I saw her gloved fingers unhooking something behind her ears, and then . . . then she caught hold of her cheeks and lifted her face clean away! The whole of that pretty face came away in her hands!

BEWARE!

It was a mask!

As she took off the mask, she turned sideways and placed it carefully upon a small table nearby, and when she turned around again and faced us, I very nearly screamed out loud.

That face of hers was the most frightful and frightening thing I have ever seen. Just looking at it gave me the shakes all over. It was so crumpled and wizened, so shrunken and shriveled, it looked as though it had been pickled in vinegar. It was a fearsome and ghastly sight. There was something terribly wrong with it, something foul and putrid and decayed. It seemed quite literally to be rotting away at the edges, and in the middle of the face, all around the mouth and cheeks, I could see the skin all cankered and worm-eaten, as though maggots were working away in there.

There are times when something is so frightful you become mesmerized by it and can't look away. I was like that now. I was transfixed. I was numbed. I was magnetized by the sheer horror of this woman's features. But there was more to it than that. There was a look of serpents in those eyes of hers as they flashed around the audience.

I knew immediately, of course, that this was none other than The Grand High Witch herself. I knew also why she had worn a mask. She could never have moved around in public, let alone book in at an hotel, with her real face. Everyone who saw her would have run away screaming.

"The doors!" shouted The Grand High Witch in a voice that filled the room and bounced around the walls. "Are they chained and bolted?"

"The doors are chained and bolted, Your Grandness," answered a voice in the audience.

BEWARE!

The brilliant snake's eyes that were set so deep in that dreadful rotting worm-eaten face glared unblinkingly at the witches who sat facing her. "You may rrree-moof your gloves!" she shouted. Her voice, I noticed, had that same hard metallic quality as the voice of the witch I had met under the conker tree, only it was far louder and much much harsher. It rasped. It grated. It snarled. It scraped. It shrieked. And it growled.

Everyone in the room was peeling off her gloves. I was watching the hands of those in the back row. I wanted very much to see what their fingers looked like and whether my grandmother had been right. Ah! . . . Yes! . . . I could see several of them now! I

could see the brown claws curving over the tips of the fingers! They were about two inches long, those claws, and sharp at the ends!

"You may rrree-moof your shoes!" barked The Grand High Witch.

I heard a sigh of relief going up from all the witches in the room as they kicked off their narrow high-heeled shoes, and then I got a glimpse under the chairs of several pairs of stockinged feet, square and completely toeless. Revolting they were, as though the toes had been sliced away from the feet with a carving knife.

"You may rrree-moof your vigs!" snarled The Grand High Witch. She had a peculiar way of speaking. There was some sort of a foreign accent there, something harsh and guttural, and she seemed to have trouble pronouncing the letter *w*. As well as that, she did something funny with the letter *r*. She would roll it round and round her mouth like a piece of hot pork crackling before spitting it out. "Rrree-moof your vigs and get some fresh air into your spotty scalps!" she shouted, and another sigh of relief arose from the audience as all the hands went up to the heads and all the wigs (with the hats still on them) were lifted away.

There now appeared in front of me row upon row of bald female heads, a sea of naked scalps, every one of them red and itchy-looking from being rubbed by the linings of the wigs. I simply cannot tell you how awful they were, and somehow the whole sight was made more grotesque because underneath those frightful scabby bald heads, the bodies were dressed in fashionable and rather pretty clothes. It was monstrous. It was unnatural.

Oh heavens, I thought. Oh help! Oh Lord have mercy on me! These foul bald-headed females are child-killers, every one of them, and here I am imprisoned in the same room and I can't escape!

At that point, a new and doubly horrifying thought struck me. My grandmother had said that with their special nose-holes they could smell out a child on a pitch-black night from right across the other side of the road. Up to now, my grandmother had been right every time. It seemed a certainty therefore that one of the witches in the back row was going to sniff me out at any moment and then the yell of "Dogs' droppings!" would go up all over the room and I would be cornered like a rat.

I knelt on the carpet behind the screen, hardly daring to breathe.

BEWARE!

Then suddenly I remembered another very important thing my grandmother had told me. "The dirtier you are," she had said, "the harder it is for a witch to smell you out."

How long since I had last had a bath?

Not for ages. I had my own room in the hotel and my grandmother never bothered with silly things like that. Come to think of it, I don't believe I'd had a bath since we arrived.

When had I last washed my hands or face?

Certainly not this morning.

Not yesterday either.

I glanced down at my hands. They were covered with smudge and mud and goodness knows what else besides.

So perhaps I had a chance after all. The stink-waves couldn't possibly get out through all that dirt.

"Vitches of Inkland!" shouted The Grand High Witch. She herself, I noticed, had not taken off either her wig or her gloves or her shoes. "Vitches of Inkland!" she yelled.

The audience stirred uneasily and sat up straight in their chairs.

"Miserable vitches!" she yelled. "Useless lazy vitches! Feeble frrribbling vitches! You are a heap of idle good-for-nothing vurms!"

A shudder went through the audience. The Grand High Witch was clearly in an ugly mood and they knew it. I had a feeling that something awful was going to happen soon.

"I am having my breakfast this morning," cried The Grand High Witch, "and I am looking out of the vindow at the beach, and vot am I seeing? I am asking you, *vot am I seeing?* I am seeing a rrree-volting sight! I am seeing hundreds, I am seeing *thousands* of rrrotten rrree-pulsive little children playing on the sand! It is

putting me rrright off my food! *Vye have you not got rrrid of them?*"
she screamed. "Vye have you not rrrubbed them all out, these
filthy smelly children?"

With each word she spoke, flecks of pale-blue phlegm shot
from her mouth like little bullets.

"I am asking you *vye!*" she screamed.

Nobody answered her question.

"Children smell!" she screamed. "They stink out the vurld!
Vee do not vont these children arrround here!"

The bald heads in the audience all nodded vigorously.

"Vun child a veek is no good to me!" The Grand High Witch
cried out. "Is that the best you can do?"

"We will do better," murmured the audience. "We will do
much better."

"Better is no good either!" shrieked The Grand High Witch.
"I demand maximum rrree-sults! So here are my orders! My
orders are that every single child in this country shall be rrrubbed
out, sqvashed, sqvirted, sqvittered, and frrrittered before I come
here again in one year's time! Do I make myself clear?"

A great gasp went up from the audience. I saw the witches all
looking at one another with deeply troubled expressions. And I
heard one witch at the end of the front row saying aloud, "*All* of
them! We can't possibly wipe out *all* of them!"

The Grand High Witch whipped around as though someone
had stuck a skewer into her bottom. "Who said that?" she

snapped. "Who dares to argue with me? It vos you, vos it not?" She pointed a gloved finger as sharp as a needle at the witch who had spoken.

"I didn't mean it, Your Grandness!" the witch cried out. "I didn't mean to argue! I was just talking to myself!"

"You dared to argue with me!" screamed The Grand High Witch.

"I was just talking to myself!" cried the wretched witch. "I swear it, Your Grandness!" She began to shake with fear.

The Grand High Witch took a quick step forward, and when she spoke again, it was in a voice that made my blood run cold.

"A stupid vitch who answers back
Must burn until her bones are black!"

she screamed.

"No, no!" begged the witch in the front row. The Grand High Witch went on:

"A foolish vitch vithout a brain
Must sizzle in the fiery flame!"

"Save me!" cried the wretched witch in the front row. The Grand High Witch took no notice of her. She spoke again:

"An idiotic vitch like you
Must rrroast upon the barbecue!"

"Forgive me, O Your Grandness!" cried the miserable culprit. "I didn't mean it!" But The Grand High Witch continued with her terrible recital:

BEWARE!

"A vitch who dares to say I'm wrrrong
Vill not be vith us very long!"

A moment later, a stream of sparks that looked like tiny
white-hot metal filings came shooting out of The Grand High
Witch's eyes and flew straight towards the one who had dared to
speak. I saw the sparks striking against her and burrowing into her
and she screamed a horrible howling scream and a puff of smoke

rose up around her. A smell of burning meat filled the room.

Nobody moved. Like me, they were all watching the smoke, and when it had cleared away, the chair was empty. I caught a glimpse of something wispy-white, like a little cloud, fluttering upwards and disappearing out of the window.

A great sigh rose from the audience.

The Grand High Witch glared around the room. "I hope nobody else is going to cross me today," she remarked.

There was a deathly silence.

"Frrrizzled like a frrritter," said The Grand High Witch. "Cooked like a carrot. You vill never see *her* again. Now vee can get down to business."

JOE IS NOT A MONSTER

by R.L. Stine

ILLUSTRATED BY TIM JACOBUS

This is the only story I ever wrote that made my son, Matt, laugh. So I *had* to include it in *Beware!*

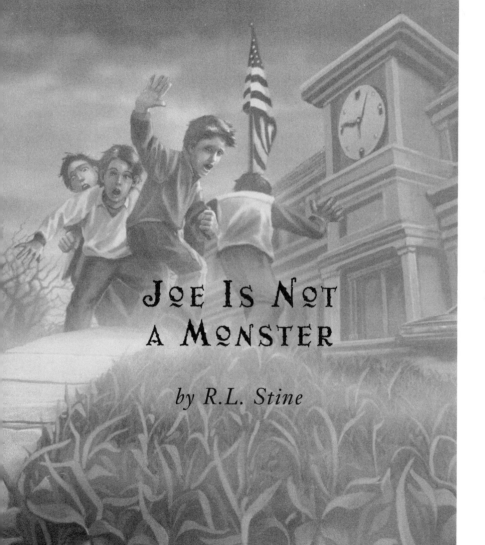

Joe Is Not a Monster

by R.L. Stine

$\mathcal{J}$oe is not a monster.

Believe me. I know Joe better than anybody.

Joe is a sweet guy. He is a pussycat. He wouldn't hurt a flea.

How did the nasty rumors get started? I really don't know.

Someone at Joe's school must have started them. Someone at Joe's school whispered to someone else that Joe was a monster. And the rumor spread and spread.

Now the whole school is against Joe.

Kids are frightened of him. Kids laugh and point at him behind his back.

The braver kids shout, "Hey, monster!" when Joe walks past. Then they laugh and hoot when they see Joe turn red.

Someone wrote "MONSTER" on Joe's locker. Someone tucked a windup toy monster in his backpack.

Because of the ugly rumors, no one will hang out with Joe. Joe eats by himself in a corner of the lunchroom.

No one will choose him for after-school soccer games. He has to stand and watch the games alone on the side of the field.

No one will dance with him at the school dances. No one even talks to him in the halls or in class.

Yesterday, a big kid from the upper school punched Joe really hard in the chest and said, "Go away from here, monster."

Joe cried all the way home.

Let me tell you something about Joe. He is very hurt by these rumors. Joe has feelings, just like everyone else.

Joe wants to have friends. He really wants people to like him.

Joe is a nice guy. He is kind and generous. He has a great sense of humor. He can be a good friend.

Joe didn't ask me to speak for him. But I am speaking out anyway. I want to set things straight once and for all.

Joe is not a monster. Not a monster. Not a monster.

How do I know so much about Joe?

Well, that question is easy to answer. No one is as close to Joe as I am. No one knows Joe better than I do.

Because I am Joe's second head.

TIGER IN THE SNOW

by Daniel Wynn Barber

ILLUSTRATED BY CHARLES BURNS

When I was a kid, sometimes I would stay at a friend's house until late and have to walk home in the dark. I lived in a quiet, peaceful neighborhood. But that walk home was always terrifying—because my imagination was *too good*!

As I hurried along the sidewalk, I would imagine a snarling wolf creature crouching behind a bush. Or a drooling fanged monster waiting to pounce from the side of a garage. Every sound made me jump. Every rustle of leaves in the wind made me think I was being followed by something hideous.

I came across this story recently and it brought back my memories of those frightening walks home. I also loved the title. Sometimes a title is so intriguing you just *have* to read the story.

In the story, Justin leaves a friend's house one night and imagines he is being followed by a *tiger*.

Is it really a tiger—or is it something even worse?

TIGER IN THE SNOW

by Daniel Wynn Barber

Justin sensed the tiger as soon as he reached the street. He didn't see it, or hear it. He simply . . . sensed it.

Leaving the warm safety of the Baxters' porch light behind him, he started down the sidewalk that fronted State Street, feeling the night swallow him in a single hungry gulp. He stopped when he reached the edge of the Baxters' property line and looked back wistfully toward their front door.

Too bad the evening had to end. It had been just about the finest evening he could remember. Not that Steve and he hadn't had some fine old times together, the way best friends will; but this particular evening had been, well, magical. They had played *The Shot Brothers* down in Steve's basement while Mr. and Mrs. Baxter watched TV upstairs. When the game had been going well and everything was clicking, Justin could almost believe that Steve and he really were brothers. And that feeling had never been stronger than it had been this evening.

When Mrs. Baxter had finally called down that it was time to go, it had struck Justin as vaguely strange that she would be packing him off on a night like this, seeing how he and Steve slept over at one another's homes just about every weekend. But this evening was different. Despite the snow, home called to him in sweet siren whispers.

Mrs. Baxter had bundled him up in his parka, boots, and mittens, and then, much to his surprise, she had kissed his cheek. Steve had seen him to the door, said a quick good-bye, then hurried away to the den. Funny thing, Steve's eyes had seemed moist.

Then Justin had stepped out into the night, and Mrs. Baxter had closed the door behind him, leaving him alone with the dark and the cold and . . . the tiger.

At the edge of the Baxters' property, Justin glanced around for a glimpse of the beast; but the street appeared deserted save for the houses and parked cars under a downy blanket of fresh snow. It was drifting down lazily now, indifferent after the heavy fall of that afternoon. Justin could see the skittering flakes trapped within the cones of light cast by the streetlamps, but otherwise the black air seemed coldly empty. The line of lamps at every corner of State Street gave the appearance of a tunnel of light that tapered down to nothingness; and beyond that tunnel, the dark pressed eagerly in.

For a moment, Justin felt the urge to scurry back to the Baxters' door and beg for sanctuary, but he knew he should be getting home. Besides, he wasn't some chicken who ran from the dark. He was one of the Shot Brothers. Rough and ready. Fearless. Hadn't he proven that to stupid Dale Corkland just the other day? "You scared?" old zit-faced Corkland had asked him. And Justin had shown him.

At the corner, Justin looked both ways, although he knew there wouldn't be many cars out on a night like this. Then he scanned the hedges along a nearby house, where dappled shadows hung frozen in the branches. Excellent camouflage for a tiger—particularly one of those white Siberian tigers he'd read about.

He kept a close eye on those hedges as he crossed the street. Snow swelled up around his boots and sucked at his feet, making it impossible to run should a tiger spring from behind the mailbox on the far corner. He stopped before he reached that mailbox, listening for the low blowing sound that tigers sometimes make as they lie in ambush. But all he heard was the rasping of his own breath. ("You scared?") Yes. Tigers were nothing to be trifled with. They were as dangerous as the ice on Shepherd's Pond.

Justin had stared at that ice, thinking about the warm weather they'd had the past week. Then he had looked up at Dale Corkland's face, three years older than his and sporting a gala display of acne. "You scared?" And Justin had shown him.

But that was then and this was now; and weren't tigers more

merciless than ice? Oh, yes indeed.

Justin gave himself a good mental shaking. He tried to summon those things his father had told him at other times when this tiger-fear had come upon him. (*Don't be such a baby.*) At night, when he would awaken screaming after a tiger nightmare. (*It was only a dream.*) Or when he felt certain that a tiger was lurking about the basement. (*There are no tigers in the city. You only find tigers in the zoo.*)

Wrapping himself snug in these assurances, Justin tramped past the brick retaining wall at the corner of State and Sixteenth without so much as a glance toward the spidery line of poplars where a tiger might be hiding. He rounded the corner and marched on. Heck, he had walked this way dozens of times. Hundreds, maybe.

But tonight the usually comfortable features seemed alien and warped out of reality under the snow, and finding himself in this strange white landscape, Justin suddenly felt the tiger-fear return. It bobbed up and down within him until he could almost feel the tiger's nearness, so close that the hot jungle breath seemed to huff against his cheek.

He was halfway down the block when he saw a shadow slip effortlessly from behind the house two doors up. It seemed to glide dreamlike across the snow, then disappear behind a car parked in the driveway. It was just a shadow, but before it had vanished, Justin thought he caught a hint of striping.

There are no tigers in the city.

Justin watched and waited—waited for whatever it was to show itself. He even considered turning back, rerouting around Rush Street, but that would put it behind him.

Come on, he scolded himself. You only find tigers in India. Or the zoo. *Or behind parked cars.* Nonsense. Tigers don't stalk kids from behind parked cars in the middle of an American city. Only little kids let themselves be scared by shadows in the night. Not one of the Shot Brothers. Not a kid who had dared the ice on Shepherd's Pond. Not a kid who was only two years away from attending Rathburn Junior High, where you get to keep your stuff in your own locker and change classrooms every hour and eat your lunch out on the benches. Kids at Rathburn didn't go whimpering and whining because they saw a shadow in the snow— probably thrown by a branch moving in the wind.

But there is no wind tonight.

Justin swallowed hard, then started forward. He walked slowly, never shifting his gaze from the taillight of that parked car. If only he could see around it without getting any nearer. If something were crouching back there, it would be on him before he could cover the first five feet. And then . . .

. . . teeth and claws, tearing and slashing.

You scared?

You bet.

When he had drawn even with the driveway across the street,

BEWARE!

Justin stopped. Two more steps, maybe three, and he would see if his father and the kids at Rathburn Junior were right, or if tigers do indeed lie in wait on winter streets. Of course, there was still time to turn back.

Perhaps it was the idea of turning back that propelled him forward. If he were to retrace his steps, he would never know; but if he looked and saw no tiger behind that car, then the tiger-fear would be banished, and he wouldn't see them anywhere. Not in bushes. Not behind trees. Not between houses. Just three steps, and he could lay tigers to rest forever.

Justin took those three steps the way he had walked out onto the ice on Shepherd's Pond. Old zit-faced Corkland had dared him, and he had faced it.

One—two—three.

He turned and looked.

Nothing. Nothing behind that car but an old sledge lying on its side. No tigers. No lions, bears, werewolves, or boogie-men. Just an old sledge. His father had been right all along.

He covered the last block and a half with steps as light and carefree as those of a June day, when the air smelled of new-mown grass and the sun baked your skin brown. But, of course, it wasn't June, and as he sprinted up his porch steps Justin realized that he had reached home without a moment to spare. He could scarcely see his breath at all. Much longer out in the icy cold and he thought his lungs might have frozen solid.

134

As he stepped into the familiar warmth of his own house, he heard voices coming from the living room. It sounded as though his folks were having a party, although the voices seemed rather subdued—much the way they sounded on bridge nights when the evenings began quietly, but noisied up as the hours grew old.

Justin tiptoed down the hall, thinking it wise not to interrupt. And as he passed the living room, he caught a snatch of conversation. It was a man speaking, ". . . bound to happen eventually. They should have put up a fence years ago. I've a good mind to . . ."

"Oh, for God's sake, Gordon," a woman said. (It sounded like Aunt Phyllis.) "This isn't the time."

That was all he heard before hurrying to his room.

When he flipped on the light, he was greeted by all the treasures which reflected his short life in intimate detail. The Darth Vader poster, the Packers pennant, the Spitfire on his dresser, the bedspread decorated in railroad logos.

And one new addition, sitting in the corner on great feline haunches.

For the briefest instant, Justin felt the urge to run—to flee into the living room and hurl himself into his mother's arms, as he had done so many times in the past. But as he stared transfixed into the tiger's huge, emerald eyes, he felt the fear slipping from him like some dark mantle, to be replaced by the soft and gentle cloak of understanding.

"It's time to go, isn't it?" he said in a voice that was low but unwavering.

The tiger's eyes remained impassive, as deep and silent as green forest pools. Warm pools that never froze over, the way Shepherd's Pond did.

In his mind, Justin heard again the pistol crack of ice giving way beneath him, and he felt the chill water closing over his head.

It really hadn't hurt that much, not the way he would have thought. Not much pain, just a moment of remorse when he realized he wouldn't be seeing his folks anymore—or Steve . . .

. . . *Had it all been a dream, this last wonderful evening together with Steve? Would Steve even remember?*

Justin looked at the tiger, searching its peaceful face for the answer; but those fathomless eyes kept their secrets.

"Did you follow me tonight?" Justin asked.

Whiskers twitched as the tiger's muzzle wrinkled into a slight grin.

"Yes," Justin said softly. "I thought it was you. You've been following me all my life, haven't you?" He turned to close his bedroom door, and when he turned back the tiger was crouching to spring.

A Sock for Christmas

A Grim Fairy Tale from The Vault of Horror, Volume 4

ILLUSTRATED BY JACK KAMEN

As a boy, I devoured horror comic books such as *Tales from the Crypt* and *The Vault of Horror*. The drawings were brilliantly gross and disgusting, and so were the stories.

Many adults thought these horror comics were bad for kids. The U.S. Congress held hearings about them and condemned them.

My mother wouldn't let me buy them. She said they were "trash." That made me like them even more. I used to go to the barbershop *every Saturday* so I could read their collection of horror comics. I had the shortest hair in America—but I never missed a single issue!

I read this story when I was ten years old, and I never forgot it. It still makes me laugh.

The drawings are by Jack Kamen, one of the master horror-comic artists. Settle back and let the Vault-Keeper give you "A Sock for Christmas."

THE VAULT-KEEPER'S
GRIM FAIRY TALE!

HEH, HEH! WELL, I SEE IT'S TIME FOR ANOTHER IDIOTIC INFANTILE INSANITY...ANOTHER CHILDISH CHILLER... ANOTHER GRIM FAIRY TALE! I'VE CHOSEN A DELIGHTFUL ONE FOR YOU THIS TIME...ONE THAT OUGHT TO TICKLE YOUR RIBS! IT'S CALLED...

A Sock for Christmas

ONCE UPON A TIME... LONG, LONG AGO... IN A HUGE BEAUTIFUL CASTLE, THERE LIVED A KING, HIS QUEEN, AND THEIR ONLY SON, THE ROYAL PRINCE! NOW, SINCE THE YOUNG PRINCE WAS THEIR ONLY SON AND HEIR TO THE THRONE, THE ROYAL COUPLE SPOILED THE BOY! WHATEVER PRINCE TARBY... FOR THAT WAS HIS NAME... WANTED, HE RECEIVED! WHATEVER HE DID WAS NEVER WRONG! AS THE KING PUT IT...

TARBY IS THE ROYAL PRINCE! HE CAN DO NO WRONG!

THE YOUNG PRINCE PUSHED ME INTO THE CASTLE MOAT, YOUR MAJESTY! IF HE WERE MY CHILD, I'D WHIP HIM BLACK AND BLUE FOR...

JACK KAMEN

THE BOY IS COMING WITH *ME*...TO THE *CASTLE!* HE WILL *LIVE* THERE... AS PRINCE TARBY'S *COMPANION!*

NO*! NO!* HE IS MY *SON!* YOU *CANNOT* TAKE HIM *FROM ME!*

WOULD YOU *DENY* YOUR SON THE ADVANTAGES I CAN *OFFER* HIM? GOOD *FOOD?* GOOD *CLOTHES?* AN *EDUCATION?*

N-NO! BUT... *BUT...*

THE COACH DOOR SWUNG OPEN...

GET *IN*, BOY*!* I *COMMAND* YOU!

THE KING *ORDERS* YOU, MY SON!

NO... SOB... FATHER... SOB...NO...

THE BOY'S FATHER PUSHED HIS YOUNG SON INTO THE COACH...

DO NOT *CRY*, SON! IT IS FOR YOUR *OWN GOOD!* WILL WE... WILL WE BE ABLE TO *SEE* HIM AGAIN, YOUR MAJESTY?

AT *CHRISTMAS!* I WILL LET HIM COME *HOME FOR CHRISTMAS!* ALL RIGHT, COACHMAN!

MAKE WAY... MAKE WAY...

THE BAKER'S SON WAS TAKEN TO THE CASTLE! BUT WHEN HE ARRIVED, HE SOON FOUND OUT THAT THERE WAS MORE TO IT THAN JUST BEING SPOILED PRINCE TARBY'S COMPANION! THERE WAS A *CATCH*...

...AND FROM *NOW ON,* LADIES AND GENTLEMEN OF THE COURT, WHEN PRINCE TARBY IS *BAD,* HE *IS* TO BE *PUNISHED!* BUT...YOU WILL NOT *WHIP* PRINCE TARBY ! YOU WILL *WHIP*...HIS *COMPANION* HERE! YOU WILL WHIP *PRINCE TARBY'S WHIPPING BOY...*

AND SO, THE FIRST *WHIPPING-BOY* CAME INTO BEING! THE POOR BAKER'S SON BECAME PRINCE TARBY'S WHIPPING SUBSTITUTE! ANYTIME TARBY WAS BAD, THE WHIPPING BOY WAS PUNISHED...

SOB... SOB...

THAT WAS...UNGG...WRONG OF YOU...UNGG...TO PUT THE... UNGG...CAT...UNGG...INTO... UNGG...THE OVEN, TARBY!

YES, ROYAL CHEF! I WON'T DO IT AGAIN, ROYAL CHEF!

NOT ONLY WAS THE WHIPPING-BOY THRASHED FOR PRINCE TARBY'S MISDOINGS! THERE WERE OTHER SUBSTITUTIONS...

WHAT DO YOU *MEAN,* YOU *HATE BATHS?* YOU'VE *GOT* TO TAKE A BATH! NOW, *COME ON...*

JUST ONE *MOMENT,* ROYAL WASHER! OH, *WHIPPING-BOY...*

YES, PRINCE TARBY!

THE WHIPPING-BOY WAS MADE TO SUBSTITUTE FOR *ALL* OF THE PRINCE'S DISTASTEFUL RESPONSIBILITIES...

SPINACH IS *GOOD* FOR YOU! YOU *MUST* EAT YOUR SPINACH, PRINCE TARBY!

YES, ROYAL DIETICIAN! ER... WHIPPING-BOY...

PASS ME YOUR *PLATE...* CHOKE... PRINCE TARBY...

SUMMER PASSED, AND FALL CAME TO THE KINGDOM! AND WITH IT CAME...

GO TO SCHOOL? I *HATE* SCHOOL! THE *ROYAL WHIPPING-BOY* WILL ATTEND *SCHOOL* FOR ME, ROYAL TUTOR! ER... *ROYAL WHIPPING-BOY...*

YES, PRINCE TARBY! WHEN DO I *START*, ROYAL TUTOR?

TOMORROW MORNING, ROYAL WHIPPING BOY! *EIGHT O'CLOCK!*

AND SO, THE WHIPPING-BOY EVEN HAD TO GO TO *SCHOOL* FOR PRINCE TARBY! THERE WASN'T *ANYTHING* THAT PRINCE TARBY DISLIKED THAT HE HAD TO DO! THE ROYAL WHIPPING BOY DID THEM *ALL...*

YOUR ROOM IS A *DISGRACE*, PRINCE TARBY! TOYS ALL *OVER!* CLEAN IT UP!

ROYAL WHIPPING BOY...

BUT WORST OF ALL WAS WHEN PRINCE TARBY WAS BAD *ON PURPOSE*...JUST TO SEE THE WHIPPING BOY RECEIVE THE WHIPPING...

AND... I HOPE...THIS...TEACHES YOU...A ...LESSON...YOUNG MAN!

SOB... SOB...

FINALLY, WINTER DREW NEAR! THE FIRST SNOW BLANKETED THE CASTLE AND THE CASTLE GROUNDS...

IT'S ALMOST *CHRISTMAS TIME,* PRINCE TARBY! SOON I WILL SEE MY *MOTHER* AND *FATHER* AGAIN...

...AND *SANTA CLAUS* WILL COME AND FILL MY *STOCKING* AND BRING ME *PRESENTS!*

...AND SANTA CLAUS WILL FILL *MY* STOCKING AND BRING *ME* PRESENTS!

HO, HO! *LISTEN* TO THE *WHIPPING-BOY!* DON'T YOU KNOW THAT SANTA CLAUS DOESN'T *BRING* THINGS TO *BAD* LITTLE BOYS?

BUT *I* HAVEN'T BEEN *BAD!* I...

YOU'VE BEEN *PUNISHED*, HAVEN'T YOU? I'VE *SEEN* IT! I'VE SEEN YOU WHIPPED A *DOZEN* TIMES OR MORE A *WEEK!* ONLY *BAD* LITTLE BOYS GET *WHIPPED!* I DON'T GET *WHIPPED!* I'M *GOOD!* SANTA WILL VISIT *ME*... NOT *YOU!*

4

FINALLY, ON THE DAY BEFORE CHRISTMAS, A COACH BROUGHT THE BAKER'S BOY...THE WHIPPING-BOY... DOWN FROM THE CASTLE TO THE VILLAGE FAR BELOW...TO THE CHILD'S MOTHER AND FATHER...

MY *BABY!* MY *BABY!*

MY *SON!*

MOMMY! DADDY! SOB... SOB...

I'LL BE BACK TO PICK HIM UP *TOMOR-ROW NIGHT!*

SOON, HE'D TOLD HIS MOTHER AND FATHER ALL ABOUT THE CASTLE AND WHY THE KING HAD BROUGHT HIM THERE...

...AND SO, IF *HE'S* BAD, I GET *WHIPPED* FOR HIM! BUT THAT DOESN'T MAKE *ME BAD, DOES* IT, FATHER... MOTHER ?

OF COURSE NOT, MY CHILD!

THE DIRTY...

...THEN SANTA CLAUS *WILL* FILL MY STOCKING...AND HE *WILL* BRING ME PRESENTS!

WELL, I... *COURSE,* MY *SON!* WHY *SHOULDN'T* HE?

OF COURSE, WE...

BECAUSE, PRINCE TARBY SAID *SANTA WOULDN'T!* HE SAID THAT *BAD* LITTLE BOYS GET *WHIPPED,* AND SINCE *I* GOT WHIPPED...

NEVER YOU *MIND,* MY *SON! GO... HANG UP A STOCK-ING...* THE *BIGGEST* ONE YOU CAN *FIND!*

AND SO, WITH TEARS OF JOY STREAMING DOWN HIS LITTLE FACE, THE ROYAL WHIPPING-BOY HUNG UP A LARGE THREADBARE STOCK-ING...

HERKIMER! YOU *KNOW* WE HAVE NO *MONEY!* HOW *COULD* WE...

HUSH, SUSQUEHANNAH! THE BOY WILL *HEAR* YOU!

THEN HE CLIMBED INTO HIS BED AND FELL FAST ASLEEP...A FAINT SMILE ON HIS TEAR-STAINED FACE...

HOW COULD YOU *PROMISE* THE BOY, HERKIMER? YOU *KNOW* WE'RE BROKE! NOW HE'LL EXPECT *SANTA CLAUS* TO *FILL* HIS STOCKING AND *GIVE* HIM PRESENTS!

THE *KING* SHOULD DO IT, SUSQUEHANNAH! THE *KING* SHOULD DO IT! AFTER ALL THAT BOY'S BEEN *THROUGH...*

...HE *OWES* IT TO HIM! THE *KING* SHOULD FILL *MELVIN'S STOCKING!* AND I'M GOING TO *ASK* HIM TO...

HERKIMER! COME *BACK!* HE'LL *LAUGH* AT YOU! HE'LL *LAUGH...*

5

THE BOY SKIPPED AND DANCED AS HE LED HIS SLEEPY-EYED PARENTS TO THE PILE OF GAYLY WRAPPED PACKAGES...

INDEED, THERE *WAS* A PRESENT FOR THE WHIPPING-BOY'S DADDY. BUT IT WAS *NOT QUITE* WHAT HE'D EXPECTED! THE *STOCKING*, HANGING OVER THE DUSTY OLD FIRE PLACE, *BULGED* STRANGELY! IT WAS *RED* AND *STICKY* AND A *SCARLET STREAM* DRIPPED FROM THE *HOLE* IN ITS TOE TO THE WORN HEARTH...

YES...HERKIMER HAD *WANTED* THE *KING* TO *FILL MELVIN'S STOCKING*, SO SANTA HAD *GIVEN* HIM WHAT HE *WANTED!*

146

THE TERRIFYING ADVENTURES OF THE GOLEM

A Jewish Folktale, retold by R.L. Stine

ILLUSTRATED BY LEO AND DIANE DILLON

The Golem is a character from Jewish folklore that has always fascinated me. I've always considered the Golem to be the first Frankenstein monster—and the first superhero. He was a giant figure made of clay and earth and water brought to life to battle the enemies of the Jewish people.

The first Golem story was told in medieval times. Whenever the Jewish people were being mistreated by the rulers where they lived, they told stories of a mighty Golem who would come to protect them.

The most famous story—which I chose to retell—relates the adventures of the Golem of Prague, brought to life in the 1500s. Yes, the story is almost five hundred years old. But I think you will agree with me that it is as exciting as any superhero adventure story told today.

THE
TERRIFYING
ADVENTURES OF
THE GOLEM

A JEWISH FOLKTALE

retold by R.L. Stine

My name is Jacob, but that is not important. This is not my story. This is the story of Rabbi Judah Levi and the terrifying creature he made to walk the earth.

Levi means *lion* in Hebrew, and it is a good name for Rabbi Levi. I am his student, and I have seen him roar many times. I have also seen his strength and his courage, and the power of his beliefs.

BEWARE!

Rabbi Levi looks like a lion with his strong, stern face, his dark eyes, and his thick mane of white hair. But he is a kind man, a wise man, and a religious man.

We Jews all need to be lions these days. We all need courage. Because the people here in the city of Prague treat us cruelly.

Yes, the emperor allows us to do business with his people. And yes, he allows us to walk the streets of Prague freely during the day.

But the Jews have a curfew. We must return to our homes in the ghetto by dark. If we are found outside our houses, we are arrested and dragged away.

My house is tiny and falling down. My three brothers and I share one room. They are younger than me and like to play and make noise. My sisters are always singing and laughing in the next room. I cannot find a quiet place to study.

I am the hotheaded one in my family. I am always the one who starts the fights with my little brothers. My mother says it is because I am a redhead. My temper is as fiery as my hair. So sometimes I complain to the Rabbi. "Why must we be forced to live on these dark, dirty streets, in these cramped, run-down houses? We have no room to breathe!"

He sighs, and I see the sadness in those deep, dark eyes.

"Jacob, it does little good to complain," he replies. "We live as well as other people."

But lately, he knows that isn't true. Everyone knows the danger we are in.

The ugly rumors have started again. People spread them all over the city.

Evil people say that the Jews kill Gentile babies. That we need their blood to make the flat bread that we eat for Passover.

The rumors are a crazy lie. Of course we do not kill babies. We love babies. We do not use blood to bake our bread.

When I heard the rumors were starting again, I became so angry, I nearly exploded. I slammed my fist into the thin wall of my room. I wanted to scream and cry out my anger.

I ran to Rabbi Levi's house. He tried to calm me down. "The rumors will pass, Jacob," he said softly, stroking his beard. "Only fools would believe such lies."

But then the rock throwing began. Chanting ugly lies, people set fire to one of our stores. A man was beaten on his way to the temple to pray.

Even the Rabbi had to admit that our lives were in danger.

"Rabbi Levi, we must get together and fight back!" I cried.

He placed a firm hand on my shoulder. "Jacob," he said, "it is not our way."

"Then what can we do?" I demanded.

He stroked his beard thoughtfully and did not reply. He paced back and forth in his small study like a caged lion. Soon, he was thinking so hard, he did not even remember that I was in the room.

Imagine my surprise when he sent for me late the next night. Imagine my amazement—and my horror—at what he had decided to do.

─◦─

The messenger told me to meet the Rabbi in the town square. He told me to bring a pack of old clothes, the biggest clothes I could find.

"But it is the middle of the night," I whispered, afraid of awakening my three brothers, who shared my bed. "Why does Rabbi Levi wish to see me now?"

The messenger raised a finger to his lips and motioned for me to hurry.

It was a cold, foggy night. The wind howled around the hunched houses of the ghetto, making shutters bang and walls creak and groan.

I gripped my bundle of old clothes tightly and ran through the cobbled street. It had rained earlier in the day, and my shoes splashed in deep puddles, sending waves of cold water up my pants legs.

By the time I reached the town square, my heart was pounding. Through the fog, I saw two figures approaching.

I held my breath. If these were the emperor's men, I'd be in terrible trouble. Jews weren't allowed out at this time of night.

I let out a sigh of relief when I recognized Rabbi Levi and my friend Isaac. Isaac is big and strong and very quiet. He studies very hard and seldom smiles. My jokes never make him laugh.

I opened my mouth to speak. But Rabbi Levi silenced me with a shake of his head. Then I realized that in his hands he carried the sacred Torah, the scrolls of Jewish wisdom and laws. "Follow me," he whispered.

Ducking our heads against the wind, we moved silently between the dark houses. The only sound was the soft splash of our shoes on the rain-wet street.

As we neared the river, I began to shiver. Not just because my coat was thin and the wind was cold. My fear grew with every step. I could not help thinking of the trouble that would follow if we were caught.

I could hear the gentle lapping of the river waters against the shore. The ground became soft. Our shoes sank into the clay of the riverbank.

The fog swirled around us, blanketing the rest of the world from view. Such an eerie silence. Such a tingling cold. I felt as if I were walking in a dream.

"We shall stop here," the Rabbi said suddenly.

He carefully set down the holy Torah scrolls and dropped to his knees. Isaac and I dropped down beside him.

BEWARE!

Without another word, Rabbi Levi dug his hands into the soft clay. He motioned for us to dig alongside him.

Even in the foggy darkness, I could see the light in the Rabbi's eyes. They burned like bright flames against the black night.

As I bent to the ground, the wind ruffled my coat, chilling the back of my neck. My hands trembled, but I forced them deep into the cold, wet clay.

Why were we digging? I dared not ask.

The Rabbi told us how to mold the clay. We were making a shape. But what kind of shape? I did not know.

"Ohh." I let out a gasp as I saw a figure begin to form. I saw arms and legs, a broad trunk, a head, long arms and legs.

It was as if the figure had risen up from the earth itself.

Shaking in fright, I stumbled back. Isaac remained bent over, his hands working the clay.

I gazed down at the clay figure—a huge man, on his back, eyes closed as if asleep.

"Rabbi, what are we doing?" I choked out.

Rabbi Levi didn't answer. He stood up, his eyes still aflame, and turned to Isaac. "Isaac, circle the shape seven times, right to left," he instructed. "And chant these words as you walk."

I watched as Isaac began to move around the clay figure, chanting the words the Rabbi told him. The fog seemed to thicken. Isaac looked as if he were a ghost, circling the clay, whispering to himself.

At last, Isaac stopped. I uttered a cry as the figure in the ground began to glow. Brighter. Brighter. Until it glowed as red as the brightest fire.

What magic is this? I wondered, frozen in fear and amazement.

Then I felt Rabbi Levi's strong hand grip my trembling shoulder. "Jacob," he whispered. "Circle the shape seven times, left to right." He told me the words to chant.

I was shaking so hard, I had to force my legs to move. Slowly at first, then faster, I began to circle the glowing mud creature.

When I stopped, my chest was heaving. Despite the cold, clinging fog, my forehead was sweating.

To my shock, the glow from the figure faded quickly. Steam hissed from the body. Water spouted from the clay like a fountain.

First fire, then water. And now black hair curled from the figure's head! I watched in awe as nails stretched from the fingers and toes.

"Rabbi—what is happening?" I finally found my voice.

"What have we done here?" Isaac asked. I could see the fear on his normally calm face.

"Do not be afraid," Rabbi Levi whispered. Then he bent over the figure. He poked his finger into the clay of its forehead.

And he wrote "EMET," the Hebrew word for *truth*.

"Come," the Rabbi instructed. He lifted the Torah scrolls into his arms. And then he led us in a slow dance, seven times around the clay creature.

When we stopped, the Rabbi quoted from the Book of Genesis: "And the Lord God . . . breathed into his nostrils the breath of life; and man became a living soul."

And the creature . . . the creature . . . *it opened its eyes!*

I couldn't stop myself. I let out a scream.

My cry was muffled by the thick fog that circled us. And by the groaning of the creature's arms and legs as he climbed to his feet.

"We have created a *golem*," the Rabbi stated.

A golem. A man who was not a man. A living creature who was not alive!

"Jacob, hand him the clothing," Rabbi Levi instructed.

But I was trembling so hard, the bundle fell from my hands. Slowly, silently, the golem bent to pick up the clothing. Quickly, he covered himself with it.

Isaac and I stumbled back. The golem was a giant. He rose up over us like a mountain. His eyes glowed like black coals. He clenched and unclenched his fists, as if testing them.

Isaac and I couldn't hide our terror. Only Rabbi Levi stood unafraid. "Golem!" he shouted up to the creature. "We have

BEWARE!

created you for one purpose—to help the Jews. You can hear but you cannot speak. You are stronger than any man. But you will use your power only at my command. You are my servant, golem. Do you understand my words?"

In reply, the golem bowed low to the Rabbi.

Rabbi Levi reached out and touched the word "EMET" on the golem's forehead. The word faded into his gray flesh. The golem stood up straight again, waiting silently for his next command.

Rabbi Levi turned to Isaac and me. He suddenly looked very tired. Wisps of wet fog clung to his beard. "No one must know what we have done here tonight," he whispered. "No one."

"But how will we hide such a giant?" I asked.

"We will not hide him," the Rabbi replied. "We will call him by the name of Joseph. I will tell everyone that I found him wandering the streets. I will take him into my house as a servant."

A red morning sun peeked over the hills. Rabbi Levi ordered the golem to follow, and we began walking toward town. The giant's heavy, plodding footsteps seemed to shake the earth. His dark eyes stared straight ahead—sad, inhuman eyes. We had to run to keep up with him.

Can such a giant truly be controlled? I wondered. I know the Rabbi is wise. But has he made a horrifying mistake tonight?

The next afternoon was bright and sunny. A cool wind brushed against my face as I made my way to the Rabbi's house. I carried my heavy books in a bag that bounced on my shoulders.

I stopped at the front door. What would I find inside? Would the golem still be there? Would he still be alive?

The Rabbi's wife opened the door and led me to Rabbi Levi's study. She shook her head and muttered to herself. "Strangers he brings into the house. Strangers who do not even speak."

Sure enough, I saw the golem sitting on a stool in a corner of the study. His huge hands rested in his lap. He stared straight ahead, not moving a muscle.

Rabbi Levi closed the door behind us and turned to me. "Are you ready for your studies, Jacob?"

"Yes, Rabbi." I sat down and began to empty my books onto the table. But I couldn't take my eyes off the golem.

Rabbi Levi rubbed his beard and gazed at the golem too. "Perhaps it is time to send Joseph outside."

He stepped up to the golem. "Joseph," he said. "Stand up."

Still staring straight ahead, the giant creature rose quickly to his feet. He had to bow his head. The ceiling was too low.

BEWARE!

"Joseph, you will go out and search the streets," the Rabbi ordered. "You will watch for trouble. You will protect our people in any way you can. You will return at sundown."

The golem didn't nod his head or blink his eyes or give any sign that he understood. He stepped past us and lumbered out of the room. I heard the front door slam behind him.

I jumped to my feet. "Rabbi, can I follow him?" I asked. "Can I see where Joseph goes?"

Rabbi Levi motioned for me to sit back down. "Jacob, the golem has his job, and you have yours. Your job is to study and become wise."

I slumped back into my seat and opened my study book. The Rabbi began his lecture, but I couldn't concentrate. I kept thinking about the giant—the giant I had helped create—and wondering what he was doing.

When my lessons were over, I thanked the Rabbi and ran out to the street. The sun had disappeared behind clouds, and the air had turned cold. My heart thudded as I made my way through the crowded, narrow streets toward the town square.

After a minute or two, I heard angry shouts and saw a small crowd of people in front of the tailor's shop. As I came closer, I saw the tailor, red-faced, shaking his fists furiously at a tall, blond man wearing a long, brown coat.

"I made the coat for you, and now you must pay for it!" the

tailor screamed, spitting the words in the man's face.

The blond man backed away, a grin on his face. "Pay a Jew?" he sneered. "You are lucky that I gave you work to keep you busy." The big coat flapping behind him, he pushed two men out of his way and stomped down the street.

But he didn't get far. The golem suddenly stepped from behind a building and blocked the blond man's path.

The crowd gasped in surprise. The tailor's mouth dropped open.

Joseph gazed down at the blond man blankly. He clenched and unclenched his big fists.

The blond man appeared lost inside Joseph's broad shadow. "L-let me pass," he stammered.

Joseph moved quickly, so quickly the crowd gasped again.

He grabbed the blond man and lifted him off the ground. Then, without any trouble at all, he turned the man upside down and began to shake him.

He shook him until the man's moneybag fell from his pocket and clattered onto the street. Joseph raised the struggling man high in one hand. Then he bent and tossed the moneybag to the tailor.

"Let me down! How dare you! Let me down!" The man struggled, kicking and thrashing his arms in the air.

Joseph let him down by tossing him through the air. The

BEWARE!

man thudded into a store wall across the street and fell to the pavement, groaning and moaning in pain.

The crowd waited until the man staggered dizzily away. Then everyone burst into applause and cheers for Joseph. They tried to clap him on the back. But they couldn't reach high enough.

The golem didn't seem to notice their excitement. He had his eyes on the sky. He saw that the sun was setting. He walked through the cheering crowd and lumbered obediently back toward the Rabbi's house.

In the next few weeks, I followed Joseph whenever I could. I stayed in the shadows and watched as he strode through the streets, dark eyes narrowed, hands lowered to his sides.

His expression wasn't angry. He didn't even appear alert. He moved as if he were sleepwalking. But when there was a problem, when one of the emperor's people tried to mistreat a Jew, Joseph sprang to action.

Some men were chanting angrily and throwing rocks at a Jewish store. Joseph stepped up to them and banged their heads together so hard, they whimpered like dogs as they staggered away. The next day, he lifted two thieves, one in each hand, and carried them to the police station.

After a short while, the streets became quiet. All was peaceful. Everyone knew that the silent giant was on patrol.

The golem was a hero. At home, my three brothers pretended

to be Joseph. They strutted around the house, acting like giants, throwing each other around.

But the peaceful times did not last long. The ugly rumors did not stop.

Ignorant, hateful people still claimed that Jews killed Gentile babies for their blood. We heard rumors that the emperor's soldiers planned to attack our ghetto.

One cold, blustery evening, I followed Joseph along the cobbled streets. Wrapping my thin coat around me, I lowered my head against a strong gust of wind.

When I raised my head, I saw that Joseph had walked up to a Gentile peddler's cart. The cart was covered by a canvas sheet. And as Joseph approached, the peddler, a short, fat man with a round, bald head, stepped away.

"What do you want?" he cried, staring up angrily at Joseph. "I have heard about you. Stay away from me. I am an honest peddler."

Joseph plucked the peddler aside as if he were a feather. Then he reached for the canvas cover on the cart.

"Stay away from there!" the peddler screamed. "I sell only apples and dried fruits. There is nothing there for you!" He tried to pull the giant away. But, of course, he hadn't the strength.

Joseph tore away the cover. He bent over the cart and picked up a large box.

BEWARE!

"Put that down! Put that down! I shall call the police!" the peddler whined.

Joseph raised the lid of the box.

Even from across the street, I could see clearly the contents of the box. My stomach lurched. I tried to cry out in horror, but only a tiny squeak escaped my mouth.

A baby. A dead baby.

The peddler was going to sneak it into the house of a Jew. And then the Jew would be blamed for killing a baby. And the emperor's soldiers would attack all of us.

My whole body was still trembling from the sight of that poor, pale little corpse. I leaned against the building to keep from falling over.

Across the street, the fat peddler tried to run away. But Joseph was too fast for him. He easily lifted the peddler off the ground and plopped him into the cart. Then he raised the whole cart over his head.

People came out of shops and houses to watch the amazing sight. Practically everyone in the ghetto followed the golem as he carried the peddler, the dead baby, and the cart. And dropped them at the police station.

Joseph was surrounded by cheering people. Once again, he was a hero. But he didn't seem to care. His expression remained as blank as ever. I watched him make his way back to the Rabbi's house as he did every evening.

Soon after that night, the emperor sent out a decree to his people. He ordered them to leave the Jews alone.

Joseph continued to patrol the streets every day. But there was little for him to do. At night, he slumped on his stool in the Rabbi's study, rested his chin in his hands, and stared blankly at the wall.

Late one night, Rabbi Levi sent for Isaac and me. "The golem has served us well," the Rabbi said softly. "Now it is time to put him to rest."

Isaac and I were both shocked. After following the golem in the streets day after day, watching his courage and strength, I had come to think of him as a human. But of course he was not human. We had brought him to life from the clay at the riverbank.

"Joseph, you will not sleep in my house tonight," the Rabbi ordered. "You will climb the stairs to the synagogue attic, and there you will make your bed."

The golem obeyed in his usual way. He made a bed of straw in the small attic and lay down on it. Rabbi Levi, Isaac, and I stood at the side of the bed.

I stared down at the golem. Pale moonlight washed in from the tiny attic window and crept over the sleeping giant's face like a soft blanket.

His arms were crossed over his broad chest. His eyelids were gently closed.

Outside, there was only silence. As if even the wind had

stopped for this moment.

A wave of sadness suddenly swept over me. Joseph had been so powerful and strong. Strong enough to defeat our enemies.

But I knew the power of God was even stronger. And the Rabbi in his wisdom was carrying out what he believed was God's wish.

Rabbi Levi ordered me to circle the sleeping golem seven times, chanting the same words as before. After I had completed the task, Isaac did the same.

"Golem, you will not wake up," Rabbi Levi ordered.

He leaned over the sleeping giant. The Hebrew word "EMET"—*truth*—appeared once again on the golem's forehead. Rabbi Levi rubbed away the first letter. And now it became the word "MET," which means *dead*.

The golem didn't stir. We covered him with the pages of old prayer books. Then we crept away. Rabbi Levi locked the attic door behind us. "The attic will be used no longer," he said.

We never spoke of the golem again.

I was but a boy when all this happened. I am an old man now. Rabbi Levi died many years ago. And Isaac moved with his family to another village.

I am the only one who remembers . . . the only one in my town who knows the truth.

I pray in the synagogue every day. And every time I enter, I think of the tiny attic room upstairs and feel a chill.

Does the golem still sleep up there?

Will someone wake him up someday?

Will Joseph walk the streets again, so brave and strong and big?

EXAMINATION DAY

by Henry Slesar

ILLUSTRATED BY PETER HORVATH

Do you get nervous before taking a test? Lots of people do. The boy in this story has good reason to be nervous!

I love stories with twist endings. Anyone who reads my books knows that I try to put some kind of twist or shock at the end of every chapter.

I read a lot of science-fiction stories and comic books when I was a kid. I liked thinking about the future, about parallel worlds, about strange ways our world might change. And I really liked the way most science-fiction stories ended with a big surprise.

Henry Slesar likes twist endings too—and the ending of this creepy story is as twisted as they come!

EXAMINATION DAY

by Henry Slesar

The Jordans never spoke of the exam, not until their son, Dickie, was twelve years old. It was on his birthday that Mrs. Jordan first mentioned the subject in his presence, and the anxious manner of her speech caused her husband to answer sharply.

"Forget about it," he said. "He'll do all right."

They were at the breakfast table, and the boy looked up from his plate curiously. He was an alert-eyed youngster, with flat blond hair and a quick, nervous manner. He didn't understand what the sudden tension was about, but he did know that today was his birthday, and he wanted harmony above all. Somewhere in the little apartment there were wrapped, beribboned packages waiting to be opened, and in the tiny wall-kitchen, something warm and sweet was being prepared in the automatic stove. He wanted the day to be happy, and the moistness of his mother's eyes, the scowl on his father's face, spoiled the mood of fluttering expectation with which he had greeted the morning.

"What exam?" he asked.

His mother looked at the tablecloth. "It's just a sort of Government intelligence test they give children at the age of twelve. You'll be getting it next week. It's nothing to worry about."

"You mean a test like in school?"

"Something like that," his father said, getting up from the table. "Go read your comic books, Dickie."

The boy rose and wandered toward that part of the living

room which had been "his" corner since infancy. He fingered the topmost comic of the stack, but seemed uninterested in the colorful squares of fast-paced action. He wandered toward the window, and peered gloomily at the veil of mist that shrouded the glass.

"Why did it have to rain *today*?" he said. "Why couldn't it rain tomorrow?"

His father, now slumped into an armchair with the Government newspaper, rattled the sheets in vexation. "Because it just did, that's all. Rain makes the grass grow."

"Why, Dad?"

"Because it does, that's all."

Dickie puckered his brow. "What makes it green, though? The grass?"

"Nobody knows," his father snapped, then immediately regretted his abruptness.

Later in the day, it was birthday time again. His mother beamed as she handed over the gaily colored packages, and even his father managed a grin and a rumple-of-the-hair. He kissed his mother and shook hands gravely with his father. Then the birthday cake was brought forth, and the ceremonies concluded.

An hour later, seated by the window, he watched the sun force its way between the clouds.

"Dad," he said, "how far away is the sun?"

"Five thousand miles," his father said.

BEWARE!

Dick sat at the breakfast table and again saw moisture in his mother's eyes. He didn't connect her tears with the exam until his father suddenly brought the subject to light again.

"Well, Dickie," he said, with a manly frown, "you've got an appointment today."

"I know, Dad. I hope—"

"Now it's nothing to worry about. Thousands of children take this test every day. The Government wants to know how smart you are, Dickie. That's all there is to it."

"I get good marks in school," he said hesitantly.

"This is different. This is a—special kind of test. They give you this stuff to drink, you see, and then you go into a room where there's a sort of machine—"

"What stuff to drink?" Dickie said.

"It's nothing. It tastes like peppermint. It's just to make sure you answer the questions truthfully. Not that the Government thinks you won't tell the truth, but this stuff makes *sure*."

Dickie's face showed puzzlement, and a touch of fright. He looked at his mother, and she composed her face into a misty smile.

"Everything will be all right," she said.

"Of course it will," his father agreed. "You're a good boy, Dickie; you'll make out fine. Then we'll come home and celebrate. All right?"

"Yes, sir," Dickie said.

They entered the Government Educational Building fifteen minutes before the appointed hour. They crossed the marble floors of the great pillared lobby, passed beneath an archway, and entered an automatic elevator that brought them to the fourth floor.

There was a young man wearing an insignia-less tunic, seated at a polished desk in front of Room 404. He held a clipboard in his hand, and he checked the list down to the Js and permitted the Jordans to enter.

The room was as cold and official as a courtroom, with long benches flanking metal tables. There were several fathers and sons already there, and a thin-lipped woman with cropped black hair was passing out sheets of paper.

Mr. Jordan filled out the form and returned it to the clerk. Then he told Dickie: "It won't be long now. When they call your name, you just go through the doorway at that end of the room." He indicated the portal with his finger.

A concealed loudspeaker crackled and called off the first name. Dickie saw a boy leave his father's side reluctantly and walk slowly toward the door.

At five minutes of eleven, they called the name of Jordan.

"Good luck, son," his father said without looking at him. "I'll call for you when the test is over."

Dickie walked to the door and turned the knob. The room inside was dim, and he could barely make out the features of the gray-tunicked attendant who greeted him.

"Sit down," the man said softly. He indicated a high stool

175

beside his desk. "Your name's Richard Jordan?"

"Yes, sir."

"Your classification number is 600-115. Drink this, Richard."

He lifted a plastic cup from the desk and handed it to the boy. The liquid inside had the consistency of buttermilk, and tasted only vaguely of the promised peppermint. Dickie downed it and handed the man the empty cup.

He sat in silence, feeling drowsy, while the man wrote busily on a sheet of paper. Then the attendant looked at his watch and rose to stand only inches from Dickie's face. He unclipped a penlike object from the pocket of his tunic and flashed a tiny light into the boy's eyes.

"All right," he said. "Come with me, Richard."

He led Dickie to the end of the room, where a single wooden armchair faced a multi-dialed computing machine. There was a microphone on the left arm of the chair, and when the boy sat down, he found its pinpoint head conveniently at his mouth.

"Now just relax, Richard. You'll be asked some questions, and you think them over carefully. Then give your answers into the microphone. The machine will take care of the rest."

"Yes, sir."

"I'll leave you alone now. Whenever you want to start, just say 'ready' into the microphone."

"Yes, sir."

The man squeezed his shoulder and left.

Dickie said, "Ready."

Lights appeared on the machine, and a mechanism whirred. A voice said:

"Complete this sequence. One, four, seven, ten . . ."

Mr. and Mrs. Jordan were in the living room, not speaking, not even speculating.

It was almost four o'clock when the telephone rang. The woman tried to reach it first, but her husband was quicker.

"Mr. Jordan?"

The voice was clipped; a brisk, official voice.

"Yes, speaking."

"This is the Government Educational Service. Your son, Richard M. Jordan, Classification 600-115, has completed the Government examination. We regret to inform you that his intelligence quotient has exceeded the Government regulation, according to Rule 84, Section 5, of the New Code."

Across the room the woman cried out, knowing nothing except the emotion she read on her husband's face.

"You may specify by telephone," the voice droned on, "whether you wish his body interred by the Government, or would you prefer a private burial place? The fee for Government burial is ten dollars."

Harold

◆

The Girl Who Stood on a Grave

retold by Alvin Schwartz
ILLUSTRATED BY GRIS GRIMLY

Alvin Schwartz collected scary stories and folktales for many years. I love his books because you can always pick one up, open it anywhere, read a short story or two, and give yourself a chill.

Some of the stories Alvin Schwartz collected have been frightening people for centuries. And they are just as scary now as the day they were first told.

Here are two of my favorites. If you have ever dared anyone to do something dangerous, you will enjoy "The Girl Who Stood on a Grave." And if scarecrows give you the creeps, don't read "Harold" late at night—or during the day, either!

HAROLD

retold by Alvin Schwartz

When it got hot in the valley, Thomas and Alfred drove their cows up to a cool, green pasture in the mountains to graze. Usually they stayed there with the cows for two months. Then they brought them down to the valley again.

The work was easy enough, but, oh, it was boring. All day the two men tended their cows. At night they went back to the tiny hut where they lived. They ate supper and worked in the garden and went to sleep. It was always the same.

Then Thomas had an idea that changed everything. "Let's make a doll the size of a man," he said. "It would be fun to make, and we could put it in the garden to scare away the birds."

"It should look like Harold," Alfred said. Harold was a farmer they both hated. They made the doll out of old sacks stuffed with straw. They gave it a pointy nose like Harold's and tiny eyes like his. Then they added dark hair and a twisted frown. Of course they also gave it Harold's name.

BEWARE!

Each morning on their way to the pasture, they tied Harold to a pole in the garden to scare away the birds. Each night they brought him inside so that he wouldn't get ruined if it rained.

When they were feeling playful, they would talk to him. One of them might say, "How are the vegetables growing today, Harold?" Then the other, making believe he was Harold, would answer in a crazy voice, "*Very* slowly." They both would laugh, but not Harold.

Whenever something went wrong, they took it out on Harold. They would curse at him, even kick him or punch him. Sometimes one of them would take the food they were eating (which they both were sick of) and smear it on the doll's face.

"How do you like that stew, Harold?" he would ask. "Well, you'd better eat it—or else." Then the two men would howl with laughter.

One night after Thomas had wiped Harold's face with food, Harold grunted.

"Did you hear that?" Alfred asked.

"It was Harold," Thomas said. "I was watching him when it happened. I can't believe it."

"How could he grunt?" Alfred asked. "He's just a sack of straw. It's not possible."

"Let's throw him in the fire," said Thomas, "and that will be that."

"Let's not do anything stupid," said Alfred. "We don't know what's going on. When we move the cows down, we'll leave him behind. For now, let's just keep an eye on him."

So they left Harold sitting in a corner of the hut. They didn't talk to him or take him outside anymore. Now and then the doll grunted, but that was all. After a few days they decided there was nothing to be afraid of. Maybe a mouse or some insects had gotten inside Harold and were making those sounds.

So Thomas and Alfred went back to their old ways. Each morning they put Harold out in the garden, and each night they brought him back into the hut. When they felt playful, they joked with him. When they felt mean, they treated him as badly as ever.

Then one night Alfred noticed something that frightened him. "Harold is growing," he said.

BEWARE!

"I was thinking the same thing," Thomas said.

"Maybe it's just our imagination," Alfred replied. "We have been up here on this mountain too long."

The next morning, while they were eating, Harold stood up and walked out of the hut. He climbed up on the roof and trotted back and forth, like a horse on its hind legs. All day and all night he trotted like that.

In the morning Harold climbed down and stood in a far corner of the pasture. The men had no idea what he would do next. They were afraid.

They decided to take the cows down into the valley that same day. When they left, Harold was nowhere in sight. They felt as if they had escaped a great danger and began joking and singing. But when they had gone only a mile or two, they realized they had forgotten to bring the milking stools.

Neither one wanted to go back for them, but the stools would cost a lot to replace. "There is really nothing to be afraid of," they told one another. "After all what could a doll do?"

They drew straws to see which one would go back. It was Thomas. "I'll catch up with you," he said, and Alfred walked on toward the valley.

When Alfred came to a rise in the path, he looked back for Thomas. He did not see him anywhere. But he did see Harold. The doll was on the roof of the hut again. As Alfred watched, Harold kneeled and stretched out a bloody skin to dry in the sun.

THE GIRL WHO
STOOD ON A GRAVE

retold by Alvin Schwartz

Some boys and girls were at a party one night. There was a graveyard down the street, and they were talking about how scary it was.

"Don't ever stand on a grave after dark," one of the boys said. "The person inside will grab you. He'll pull you under."

"That's not true," one of the girls said. "It's just a superstition."

"I'll give you a dollar if you stand on a grave," said the boy.

"A grave doesn't scare me," said the girl. "I'll do it right now."

The boy handed her his knife. "Stick this knife in one of the graves," he said. "Then we'll know you were there."

The graveyard was filled with shadows and was as quiet as death. "There is nothing to be scared of," the girl told herself, but she was scared anyway.

BEWARE!

She picked out a grave and stood on it. Then quickly she bent over and plunged the knife into the soil, and she started to leave. But she couldn't get away. Something was holding her back! She tried a second time to leave, but she couldn't move. She was filled with terror.

"Something has got me!" she screamed, and she fell to the ground.

When she didn't come back, the others went to look for her. They found her body sprawled across the grave. Without realizing it, she had plunged the knife through her skirt and had pinned it to the ground. It was only the knife that held her. She had died of fright.

A Grave Misunderstanding

by Leon Garfield

ILLUSTRATED BY BLEU TURRELL

I love dogs. My dog, Nadine, keeps me company all day. She sleeps under my desk while I'm writing.

I've written lots of scary stories about dogs. I've written about ghost dogs and evil dogs and missing dogs and monster dogs.

There's an old belief that dogs have a special ability—that they can always sense when a ghost is nearby. I don't know if it's true or not, but it certainly makes for good, scary stories.

I picked this story because it's actually *told* by a dog. It's a funny story, but there is a very scary idea behind it. After all, if you were a dog, what would you do if you ran into a ghost?

A GRAVE
MISUNDERSTANDING

by Leon Garfield

I am a dog. I think you ought to know right away. I don't want to save it up for later, because you might begin to wonder what sort of person it was who went about on all fours, sniffing at bottoms and soiling lampposts in the public street. You wouldn't like it, and I don't suppose you'd care to have anything more to do with me.

The truth of the matter is we have different standards, me and my colleagues, that is; not in everything, but in enough for it to be noticeable. For instance, although we are as fond of a good walk as the next person, and love puppies and smoked salmon, we don't go much on reading. We find it hard to turn the pages. But, on the other paw, a good deep snoutful of mingled air as it comes humming off a garbage dump can be as teasing to us as a sonnet. Indeed, there are rhymes in rancid odors such as you'd never dream of, and every puddle tells a story.

BEWARE!

We see things, too. Only the other day, when me and my Person were out walking through that green and quiet place of marble trees and stony, lightless lampposts, where people bury their bones and never dig them up, I saw a ghost. I stopped. I glared, I growled, my hair stood up on end—

"What the devil's the matter with you now?" demanded my Person.

"What a beautiful dog!" said the ghost, who knew that I knew what she was, and that we both knew my Person did not.

She was the lifeless, meaningless shell of a young female person whose bones lay not very far away. No heart beat within her, there was wind in her veins, and she smelled of worm crumble and pine.

"Thank you," said my Person, with a foolish smile, for the ghost's eyes were very come-hitherish, even though her hither was thither, under the grass. "He *is* rather a handsome animal. Best of breed, you know." The way to his heart was always open through praise of me.

"Does he bite?" asked the ghost, watching me with all the empty care of nothingness trying to be something.

"SHE'S DEAD—SHE'S DEAD!"

"Stop barking!" said my Person. "Don't be frightened. He wouldn't hurt a fly. Do you come here often?"

"Every day," murmured the ghost, with a sly look toward her bones. She moved a little nearer to my Person. A breeze sprang up, and I could smell it blowing right through her, like frozen flowers. "He looks very fierce," said the ghost. "Are you sure that he's kind?"

"COME AWAY—COME AWAY!"

"Stop barking!" commanded my Person, and he looked at the ghost with springtime in his eyes. If only he could have smelled the dust inside her head and heard the silence inside her breast! But it was no good. All he could see was a silken smile. He was only a person and blindly trusted his eyes. . . .

"Dogs," said the ghost, "should be kept on a leash in the churchyard. There's a notice on the gate." She knew that I knew where she was buried and that I'd just been going to dig up her bones.

My Person obeyed, and the ghost looked at me as if to say, "Now you'll never be able to show him that I'm dead!"

"SHE'S COLD! SHE'S EMPTY! SHE'S GRAND-DAUGHTER DEATH!"

"Stop barking!" shouted my Person, and dragging me after, he walked on, already half in love with the loveless ghost.

We passed very close to her bones. I could smell them, and I could hear the little nibblers dryly rustling. I pulled, I strained, I jerked to dig up her secret. . . .

"He looks so wild!" said the ghost. "His eyes are rolling, and his jaws are dripping. Are you sure he doesn't have a fever? Don't you think he ought to go to the vet?"

BEWARE!

"He only wants to run off and play," said my Person. "Do you live near here?"

"YES! YES! RIGHT THERE! SIX PAWS DEEP IN THE EARTH!"

"Stop barking!" said my Person. "Do you want to wake up the dead?"

The ghost started. Then she laughed, like the wind among rotting leaves. "I have a room nearby," she murmured. "A little room all to myself. It is very convenient, you know."

"A little room all to yourself?" repeated my Person, his heart beating with eager concern. "How lonely that must be!"

"Yes," she said. "Sometimes it is very lonely, even though I hear people walking and talking upstairs, over my head."

"Then let me walk back with you," said my Person, "and keep you company!"

"No dogs allowed," said the ghost. "They would turn me out, you know."

"Then come my way!" said my Person, and the ghost raised her imitation eyebrows in imitation surprise. "'Madam, will you walk,'" sang my Person laughingly. "'Madam, will you talk, Madam, will you walk and talk with me?'"

"I don't see why not," smiled the ghost.

"BECAUSE SHE'S DEAD—DEAD—DEAD!"

"Stop barking!" said my Person. "'I will give you the keys of Heaven, I will give you the keys of my heart . . .'"

"The keys of Heaven?" sighed the ghost. "Would you really?"

"And the keys of my heart! Will you have dinner with me?"

"Are you inviting me into your home?"

"NO GHOSTS ALLOWED! SHE'LL TURN ME OUT!"

"Stop barking! Yes . . . if you'd like to!"

"Oh, I would indeed—I would indeed!"

"DON'T DO IT! YOU'LL BE BRINGING DEATH INTO OUR HOME!"

"Stop that barking! This way . . . this way. . . ."

It was hopeless, hopeless! There was only one thing left for a dog to do. *She* knew what it was, of course. She could see it in my eyes. She walked on the other side of my Person and always kept him between herself and me. I bided my time. . . .

"Do you like Italian food?" asked my Person.

"Not spaghetti," murmured the ghost. "It reminds me of worms."

It was then that I broke free. I jerked forward with all my strength and wrenched the leash out of my Person's grasp. He shouted! The ghost glared and shrank away. For a moment I stared into her eyes, and she stared into mine.

"Dogs must be kept on a leash!" whispered the ghost as I jumped. "There's a notice on . . . on . . . on . . ."

It was like jumping through cobwebs and feathers, and when I turned, she'd vanished like a puff of air. I saw the grass shiver,

BEWARE!

and I knew she'd gone back to her bones.

"SHE WAS DEAD! SHE WAS DEAD! I TOLD YOU SO!"

My Person didn't answer. He was shaking. He was trembling. For the very first time, he couldn't believe his eyes.

"What happened? Where—where is she? Where has she gone?"

I showed him. Trailing my leash, I went to where she lay, six paws under, and began to dig.

"No! No!" he shrieked. "Let her lie there in peace!"

Thankfully, I stopped. The earth under the grass was thick and heavy, and the going was hard. I went back to my Person. He had collapsed on a bench and was holding his head in his hands. I tried to comfort him by licking his ear.

A female person walked neatly by. She was young and smooth and shining and smelled of coffee and cats. She was dressed in the softest of white.

"Oh, what a beautiful dog," she said, pausing to admire me.

He stared up at her. His eyes widened. His teeth began to chatter. He could not speak.

"GO ON! GO ON! 'BEST OF BREED'!"

"Hush!" said the female person with a gentle smile. "You'll wake up the dead!"

"Is she real?" whispered my Person, his eyes as wide and round as plates. "Or is she a ghost? Show me, show me! Try to jump through her like you did before! Jump, jump!"

"BUT SHE'S REAL! SHE'S ALIVE!"

"Stop barking and jump!"

So I jumped. She screamed—but not in fright. She screamed with rage. My paws were still thick and filthy with churchyard mud, and in a moment, so was her dress.

"You—you madman!" she shouted at my shamefaced Person. "You told him to do it! You told him to jump! You're not fit to have a dog!"

"But—but—" he cried out as she stormed away to report him, she promised, to the churchyard authorities and the ASPCA.

"I TOLD YOU SHE WAS ALIVE! I TOLD YOU SO!"

"Stop barking!" wept my Person. "Please!"

MISTER ICE COLD

by Gahan Wilson

ILLUSTRATED BY GAHAN WILSON

Gahan Wilson is one of my favorite cartoonists. I have been laughing at his magazine cartoons for a long time. He has an evil sense of humor. His cartoons make you laugh—and shudder—at the same time.

I was very happy when I found some stories written by Gahan Wilson. I knew they would have the quality of being scary and funny at the same time.

This one is my favorite. It seems innocent at first—almost sweet. What could be sweeter than the jingle-jangle of an ice cream truck's bell on a hot summer day?

But watch out. This story is truly ghastly. Trust me—it's evil and disgusting, *and* it will make you laugh!

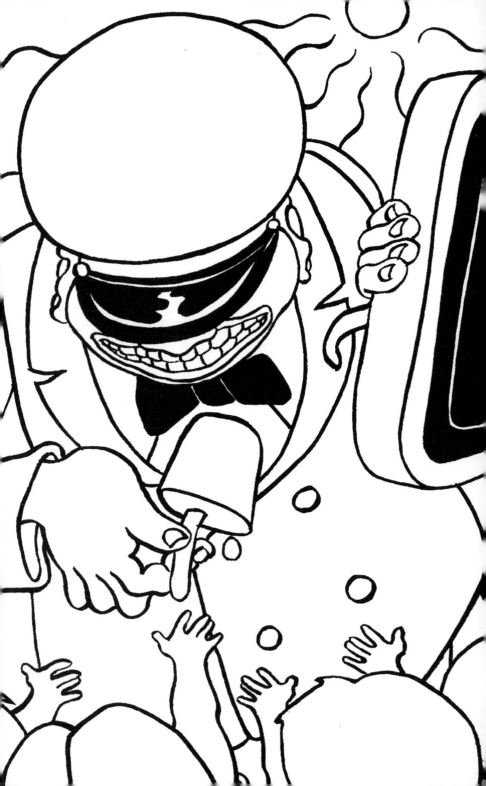

MISTER ICE COLD

by Gahan Wilson

Listen, children! Hear the music? Hear its bright and cheerful chiming coming down the street? Hear it playing its pretty little tune—*dingy di-ding, dingy di-ding*—as it sings softly through the green trees, through the blue sky overhead, as it sings through the thick, still, sultry summer heat?

It's Mister Ice Cold coming in his truck! Mister Ice Cold and his nice ice cream! Fat, round, cool balls of it plopped into cones! Thick, juicy slabs of it covered in frozen chocolate frosting and stuck on sticks! Soft, pink, chilly twirls of it oozed into cups!

The music's coming closer through the heat—*dingy di-ding, dingy di-ding*—and excitement starts stirring where all was lazy and drowsy just a sweaty blink before!

Bobby Martin's no longer lying flat on the grass, staring up at a slow-moving summer cloud without seeing it at all; he's scrambled to his feet and is running over the thick summer grass to ask

BEWARE!

his mother—nodding on the porch over a limp magazine almost slipped from her fingers—if he can have enough money to buy a frozen lime frog.

And Suzy Brenner's left off dreamily trying to tie her doll's bonnet over her cat's head (much to the cat's relief) and is desperately digging into her plastic, polka-dot purse to see if there's enough change in there to buy her a cup of banana ice cream with chocolate sprinkles. Oh, she can taste the sweetness of it! Oh, her throat can feel its coolness going down!

And you, you've forgotten all about blowing through a leaf to see if you can make it squeak the way you saw Arnold Carter's older brother do it; now you're clawing feverishly with your small hands in both pockets, feeling your way past that sandy shell you found yesterday on the beach, and that little ball chewed bounceless by your dog, and that funny rock you came across in the vacant lot which may, with luck, be full of uranium and highly radioactive, and so far you have come up with two pennies and a quarter and you think you've just touched a nickel.

Meantime Mister Ice Cold's truck is rolling ever closer—*dingy di-ding, dingy di-ding*—and Martin Walpole, always a show-off, wipes his brow, points, and calls out proudly: "I see it! There it is!"

And, sure enough, *there it is*, rolling smoothly around the corner of Main and Lincoln, and you can see the shiny, fat fullness of its white roof gleaming in the bright sun through the thick, juicy-green foliage of the trees which have, in the peak of their summer swelling, achieved a tropical density and richness more appropriate to some Amazonian jungle than to midwestern Lakeside, and you push aside one last, forgotten tangle of knotted string in your pocket and your heart swells for joy because you've come across another quarter and that means you've got enough for an orange icicle on a stick which will freeze your fillings and chill your gut and stain your tongue that gorgeous, glowing copper color which never fails to terrify your sister!

Now Mister Ice Cold's truck has swept into full view and its *dingy di-ding* sounds out loud and clear and sprightly enough, even in this steaming, muggy air, to startle a sparrow and make it swerve in its flight.

Rusty Taylor's dog barks for a signal and all of you come running quick as you can from every direction, coins clutched in your sweaty fingers and squeezed tightly as possible in your damp, small palms, and every one of you is licking your lips and staring at the bright-blue lettering painted in frozen ice cubes and spelling out MISTER ICE COLD over the truck's sides and front and back, and Mister Ice Cold himself gives a sweeping wave of his big, pale hand to everyone from behind his wheel and brings his vehicle and all the wonders it contains to a slow, majestic halt with the skill and style of a commodore docking an ocean liner.

"A strawberry rocket!" cries fat Harold Smith, who has got there way ahead of everyone as usual, and Mister Ice Cold flips open one of the six small doors set into the left side of the truck with a *click* and plucks out Harold's rocket and gives it to him and takes the money, and before you know it he has smoothly glided to the right top door of the four doors at the truck's back and opened it, *click*, and Mandy Carter's holding her frozen maple tree and licking it and handing her money over all at the same time, and now Mister Ice Cold is opening one of the six small doors on the right side of the truck, *click*, and Eddy Morse has bitten the point off the top of his bright red cinnamon crunchy munch and is completely happy.

Then your heart's desire is plucked with a neat *click* from the top middle drawer on the truck's right side, which has always been its place for as long as you can remember, and you've put your money into Mister Ice Cold's large, pale, always cool palm, and as you step back to lick your orange icicle and to feel its coolness trickle down your throat, once again you find yourself admiring the sheer athletic smoothness of Mister Ice Cold's movements as he glides and dips, spins and turns, bows and rises, going from one small door, *click*, to another, *click*, with never a stumble, *click*, never a pause, *click*, his huge body leaving a coolness in the wake of his passing, and you wish you moved that smoothly when you ran back over the gravel of the playground with your hands stretched up, hoping for a catch, but you know you don't.

Everything's so familiar and comforting: the slow quieting of the other children getting what they want, your tongue growing ever more chill as you reduce yet another orange icicle, lick by lick, down to its flat stick, and the heavy, hot summer air pressing down on top of it all.

But this time it's just a little different than it ever was before because, without meaning to, without having the slightest intention of doing it, you've noticed something you never noticed before. Mister Ice Cold never opens the bottom right door in the back of the truck.

He opens all the rest of them, absolutely every one, and you see him doing it now as new children arrive and call out what they want. *Click, click, click,* he opens them one after the other, producing frozen banana bars and cherry twirls and all the other special favorites, each one always from its particular, predictable door.

But his big, cool hand always glides past that *one door* set into the truck's back, the one on the bottom row, the one to the far right. And you realize now, with a funny little thrill, that you have never—not in all the years since your big brother Fred first took you by the hand and gave Mister Ice Cold the money for your orange icicle because you were so small you couldn't even count—you have never *ever* seen that door open.

And now you've licked the whole orange icicle away, and your tongue's moving over and over the rough wood of the stick without feeling it at all, and you can't stop staring at that door, and you know, deep in the pit of your stomach, that you have to open it.

BEWARE!

You watch Mister Ice Cold carefully now, counting out to yourself how long it takes him to move from the doors farthest forward back to the rear of the truck, and because your mind is racing very, very quickly, you soon see that two orders in a row will keep him up front just long enough for you to open the door which is never opened, the door which you are now standing close enough to touch, just enough time to take a quick peek and close it shut before he knows.

Then Betty Deane calls out for a snow maiden right on top of Mike Howard's asking for a pecan pot, and you know those are both far up front on the right-hand side.

Mister Ice Cold glides by you close enough for the cool breeze coming from his passing to raise little goose bumps on your arms. Without pausing, without giving yourself a chance for any more thought, you reach out.

Click!

Your heart freezes hard as anything inside the truck. There, inside the square opening, cold and bleached and glistening, are two tidy stacks of small hands, small as yours, their fingertips reaching out toward you and the sunlight, their thin, dead young arms reaching out behind them, back into the darkness. Poking over the top two hands, growing out of something round and shiny and far back and horribly still, are two stiff golden braids of hair with pretty frozen bows tied onto their ends.

But you have stared too long in horror and the door is closed, *click*, and almost entirely covered by Mister Ice Cold's hand, which now seems enormous, and he's bent down over you with his huge, smiling face so near to yours you can feel the coolness of it in the summer heat.

"Not that door," he says, very softly, and his small, neat, even teeth shine like chips from an iceberg, and because of his closeness now you know that even his breath is icy cold. "Those in there are not for you. Those in there are for me."

Then he's standing up again and moving smoothly from door to door, *click*, *click*, *click*, and none of the other children saw inside, and none of them will really believe you when you tell them, though their eyes will go wide and they'll love the story, and not a one of them saw the promise for you in Mister Ice Cold's eyes.

But you did, didn't you? And some night, after the end of summer, when it's cool and you don't want it any cooler, you'll be lying in your bed all alone and you'll hear Mister Ice Cold's pretty little song coming closer and closer through the night, through the dead, withered autumn leaves.

Dingy di-ding, dingy di-ding . . .

Then, later on, you just may hear the first *click*.

But you'll never hear the second *click*.

None of them ever do.

Haunted

◆

Blood-Curdling Story

by Shel Silverstein

ILLUSTRATED BY SHEL SILVERSTEIN

No one makes me laugh like Shel Silverstein. I don't know which is funnier—his poems or the crazy pictures he drew to go with them.

The first Shel Silverstein book I ever saw was called *Uncle Shelby's ABZ Book*. It had to be the strangest, most twisted ABC book ever written—definitely not for kids!

After that, I looked forward to each new book of his poems. You might not think of Shel's work as scary. But here are two poems I love because they have twist endings—which isn't easy to do in a very short poem!

HAUNTED

by Shel Silverstein

I dare you all to go into
The Haunted House on Howlin' Hill,
Where squiggly things with yellow eyes
Peek past the wormy window sill.
We'll creep into the moonlit yard,
Where weeds reach out like fingers,
And through the rotted old front door
A-squeakin' on its hinges,
Down the dark and whisperin' hall,
Past the musty study,
Up the windin' staircase—
Don't step on the step that's bloody—
Through the secret panel
To the bedroom where we'll slide in
To the ragged cobweb dusty bed
Ten people must have died in.
And the bats will screech,
And the spirits will scream,
And the thunder will crash
Like a horrible dream,
And we'll sing with the zombies
And dance with the dead,
And howl at the ghost
With the axe in his head,
And—come to think of it what do you say
We go get some ice cream instead?

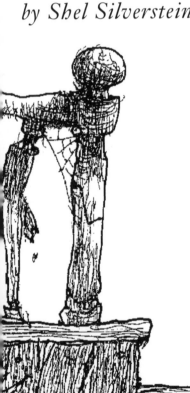

Blood~Curdling Story

by Shel Silverstein

That story is creepy,
It's waily, it's weepy,
It's screechy and screamy
Right up to the end.
It's spooky, it's crawly,
It's grizzly, it's gory,
It's the *awfulest* story
(Please tell it again).

R.L. (ROBERT LAWRENCE) STINE is one of the best-selling children's authors in history. He began his writing career at the age of nine, writing short stories, joke books, and comic books for his friends—and has been at it ever since!

After graduating from Ohio State University, R.L. moved to New York to become a writer. He wrote dozens of joke books and humor books for young people, and created *Bananas*, a zany humor magazine. In 1989, R.L. turned scary. He teamed up with Parachute Press to create *Fear Street*, which soon became the best-selling young adult series in the nation. In 1992, Stine and Parachute went on to launch *Goosebumps*, the phenomenal series that made R.L. an international celebrity and the number-one best-selling children's author of all time (*Guinness Book of World Records*).

His two original collections of scary stories, the *New York Times* best-seller *Nightmare Hour* and *The Haunting Hour*, have won R.L. legions of new fans. His book series The Nightmare Room, also published by HarperCollins, was adapted into a popular TV series.

R.L. Stine lives in Manhattan with his wife, Jane, and their son, Matthew.

"The Black Ferris" by Ray Bradbury reprinted by permission of Don Congdon Associates, Inc. Copyright © 1948 by *Weird Tales*, renewed 1975 by Ray Bradbury. "The Conjure Brother" from *The Dark Thirty* by Patricia McKissack, illustrated by Brian Pinkney, text copyright © 1992 by Patricia C. McKissack. Illustrations copyright © 1992 by Brian Pinkney. Used by permission of Alfred A. Knopf Children's Books, a division of Random House, Inc. "My Sister Is a Werewolf" text copyright © 1996 by Jack Prelutsky. Used by permission of HarperCollins Publishers. "The Elevator" copyright © 1989 by William Sleator. All rights reserved. Used with permission. "The Meeting" and "Frizzled Like a Fritter" from *The Witches* by Roald Dahl. Copyright © 1983 by Roald Dahl. Illustrations copyright © 1983 by Quentin Blake. Reprinted by permission of Farrar, Straus and Giroux, LLC. "A Sock for Christmas" copyright © William M. Gaines, Agent, Inc. Incl. 1952. Used by permission. All rights reserved. "Examination Day" copyright © 1994 by Henry Slesar. Published by arrangement with Henry Slesar. "Harold" copyright © 1991 by Alvin Schwartz. Used by permission of HarperCollins Publishers. "The Girl Who Stood on a Grave" copyright © 1981 by Alvin Schwartz. Used by permission of HarperCollins Publishers. "A Grave Misunderstanding" copyright © The Estate of Leon Garfield 2002, reprinted by permission of John Johnson Ltd, London. "Mister Ice Cold" (text and illustration) copyright © 1990, originally published in *OMNI* by arrangement with Gahan Wilson. Permission granted by the author and the author's agents, The Pimlico Agency, Inc. "Haunted" and "Blood-Curdling Story" from *Falling Up* by Shel Silverstein. Copyright © 1996 by Evil Eye Music, Inc. Used by permission of HarperCollins Publishers.

Every effort has been made to obtain permission to reprint the other stories in this volume. If necessary, the publisher will add the proper credit in future printings.